THE CHILDREN OF ENOCH

DARK HARVEST

A NEW BABEL BOOKS RELEASE

EDWARD GEHLERT

A New Babel Books Release 381 High Point Drive Holiday Shores, IL 62025

Genre: Horror / Series
ISBN: 978-1-63196-027-7
First Edition.
Printed in the United States of America.

Praise for *Children of Enoch: Dark Harvest*

"Edward Gehlert's novel is a bold statement in a world full of politically correct nonsense. The story grabs you like a mugger and does not let go until it has gotten every bit of emotion you have to give. I look forward to future novels from Mr. Gehlert and cannot wait to continue the thrill-ride that is the *Children of Enoch* series."

> \- Corey A. Phillips, Director of Zombification,
> Orientation & Defense (Z.O.D.)

"Edward's writing takes you back to a time that will feel so familiar. Times that are so peaceful and happy that you think things will never change. A place you loved to be and then, in an instant, he takes you to a place you're glad you never were and hope to God you will never be! His meticulous attention to details are puzzle pieces to this story your imagination won't have to find. I won't guarantee a happy ending, but I'll guarantee you'll be happy you read it."

> \- Nathan Shaw, Co-Host Brothers on Whatever

"Edward Gehlert's characters grab you with such intensity that you feel as though they are family; family that you want to protect and help along on their journey. And a journey they have! If this is to be the first of many from the author, I'll definitely be in line for the next."

> \- James Craigmiles, Actor and Author of First, Last, Only...

"*Children of Enoch* is a suspenseful page-turner that deals with the dark side of human nature. As Gehlert sets up the characters, he paints a picture of human nature that is selfish, violent and hateful. As the book evolves into the main event, that human nature is not changed, but accentuated. This book illustrates a dynamic between the sins of selfish indifference and the more violent sins of a world gone awry. Are our sins any more forgivable because they function within the confines of societal acceptance? This book tells us what happens when that societal structure falls apart- all that is left are the sins that cause us to function at an autonomous "reptile brain" level."

> \- Rev. Rick Oberle, United Church of Christ

This is for Eva and Jason. Thank you both for helping me believe I can do great things. Thank you even more for putting up with me over the years. I love you both more than you will ever know.

Wayde, follow your dreams and find your own road less travelled.

CONTENTS

FOREWORD

When Ed came to me about writing a franchise novel in *The Apocalypse of Enoch* world setting, I was hesitant. Here was a writer who specialized in technical manuals and guide books, but that had never written anything in this genre before. I almost declined his proposition; however I saw he had a passion for the world setting.

So, I said to him send me 300 words ...and he did. And while there were some typical issues associated with a writer who was accustomed to more technical works (Telling not showing, passive voice, and dialog tags all over the place) I saw something. Something that was wonderfully horrible. Something so brilliantly nasty…

I spent some time with him behind the scenes and when I was happy with the plot, I unleashed his twisted mind upon the world of Enoch. ...and oh how nasty he had become. *Children of Enoch: Dark Harvest* was born. Grab a glass of water and some covers to hide under. You're going to need it.

- Shane Moore, Best Selling Author of The Apocalypse of Enoch series.

ACKNOWLEDGMENTS

After many years in the publishing industry, a random meeting reminded me why I fell in love with writing in the first place. Shane Moore, author of many wonderful books, reignited my love of fiction with his novel *The Apocalypse of Enoch*.

From that chance meeting, a business relationship developed that evolved into friendship. I would like to thank him for the many worlds he has conjured and for the opportunity he has given me to create my own little slices of sci-fi in those realities.

I would also like to thank the amazing people at New Babel Books, New Babel Distribution, and F&M Publishing. They are very dedicated to their work and demand the same dedication from others on their team. This has helped push me to new levels and I continue to grow because of them.

This book would not be in publication without the hard work and expertise of the amazingly talented Kendall R. Hart. He is a man who, in my opinion, is truly the definition of the word artist.

Speaking of artists, a special thank you needs to go out to Terry Naughton. This is a man who gives so selflessly of his time to help out young artists. My family and I truly are blessed to call him friend.

In closing, I want to thank Kevin Smith. I have never met him, but he has had an impact on my life. He dared to risk everything for something he believed in. He rolled the dice and won. I'm glad he is a gambler. It gives me hope for my future… Come on lucky 7!

THE CHILDREN
OF ENOCH

DARK HARVEST

"For I have chosen him, that he may command his children and his household after him to keep the way of the Lord by doing righteousness and justice, so that the Lord may bring to Abraham what he has promised him."

- Genesis 18:19

STICKS & STONES

Hannibal, Missouri – Seven Years Ago

Joey and his younger brother Sean ambled along the banks of the Mississippi River enjoying the weather. The smell of the water invigorated and energized the young boys as they played. As the temperature gradually warmed, they had been able to convince their mother they didn't need to wear windbreakers anymore. She grudgingly gave them permission to remove the jackets, only forcing them to put the apparel on because of the cold snap that slipped in that morning anyway.

Joey tied his jacket around his waist, giving him full use of his arms and hands to poke and prod his younger brother. Sean had initially tied his jacket as well, but when his brother started aggravating him he used it as a makeshift defense against the abuse. He did his best to dodge his older brother's mistreatment and occasionally managed to avoid some of the torment. Joey cuffed him on the side of his head with his jacket with enough force to cause his head to turn. From his new field of vision Sean noticed a strange pile of rocks further down the trail. He tossed his jacket to his mom with wild abandon before running up to investigate.

Joey raced after his brother when he bolted away, snatching up a stick from the ground as he went. He swung it back and forth a few times and when he got close to his brother he began poking him in the back with it. Sean was completely engrossed in examining the strange pile and didn't seem to notice what Joey was doing for a few seconds.

"Momma, make him stop!"

"Momma, make him stop," teased Joey, though he did pull the stick away from his brother when he noticed the glare his mother gave him.

Mary shook her head as she watched her sons bicker back and forth. She was a young mother, having gotten pregnant with Joey when she was sixteen and had him just a month shy of her seventeenth birthday. She ended up marrying his father shortly after the boy's second birthday.

He had proposed to her when they found out that she was pregnant with another child after Joey turned just over a year old. She had lost the baby a few months into the pregnancy, but the young couple decided to go ahead with the marriage anyway. After all, they were in love and had a bright future.

"Momma, come see!" squealed Sean with excitement, breaking her out of her thoughts.

"What is it, Hun?"

"It's just a pile of sticks and rocks!" called out Joey from beside his brother.

Mary chuckled and moved toward her sons. Sean had always been excitable and so full of wonder with the world around him. It was nice to see that he hadn't lost any of that fascination after celebrating his sixth birthday earlier in the month.

When she looked at her youngest boy, and especially when she looked into those bright green eyes of his, she always felt a little out of place and uneasy. She loved him, that was certain, but when she had originally found out she was pregnant with him she had seriously considered having an abortion.

The timing of her pregnancy had been all wrong. Things

had soured between her and Doug, the boy's father. When she found out he was cheating on her, she decided to return the favor. After a few months of both of them sneaking around on each other, Mary had decided to call it quits.

The day she was going to meet the lawyer to file paperwork was the same day morning sickness hit her. She couldn't remember how long she had cried when the test she took came back positive, but she did remember the angry look Doug gave her and the heated words.

They both decided to stick it out until after the baby was born and paternity was proven. If it was his, they would try to reconcile and, if not, the divorce would certainly proceed. During that time, things had become so cold around the house that Mary kept entertaining the idea of abortion just so she could get away from Doug. Even little Joey knew that something was wrong between Momma and Daddy.

She felt guilty every time she thought about how much she almost had given up, and at times like this when Sean smiled up at her and moved his red hair out of his eyes, she felt choked up.

"Show Momma what you found," she said, managing to keep the catch out of her throat.

"I told you it's just a pile of sticks and rocks, Mom," Joey said under his breath.

"Nuh-uh Joey, it's something special. Someone made it," countered Sean.

Mary knelt down and examined the pile her son had found. She noticed that the rocks were all different shapes and sizes and it looked like the sticks had been placed in an "x" pattern between the various layers of rocks and dirt.

"This wasn't here last week," she remarked.

"No, it wasn't. I would of 'membered," Sean said proudly.

"Who cares? It's just a stupid pile of dirt and rocks," his older brother said while stepping on Sean's foot.

"Momma, he's getting my shoe dirty!"

Mary wasn't listening to the bickering of her children anymore. The size of the pile is what intrigued her most. It was roughly three foot high and had a diameter of at least five feet. The placement of the sticks, small branches really, started at the base of the mound and contained another cross section in the middle with one more on top. The top branches were tied together with what appeared to be hair.

The smell of freshly dug earth was heavy in the air and there was another odor, very faint, that Mary couldn't place. The wind picked up, causing a chill to run all over her body and she hugged Sean's windbreaker closer to her chest. The sound of the wind moving among the fall trees made an eerie wail that sent a shudder through her spine. A shudder that intensified when she realized that, other than the wind and the ripples on the shore of the Mississippi, there were no other noises coming from the forest.

"Momma?" she heard Sean ask.

"Put your jackets back on," she said as she handed Sean his windbreaker.

"But—" began Joey.

"No 'buts' now. Get your jacket back on, we're goin' home," she said with a tone of finality.

"We can't dig in the pile?" asked Sean, sounding disappointed.

Mary felt a sense of dread when he asked her that question. The thought of disturbing the pile really bothered her, although she had no idea why. She could also tell that Joey didn't want to have anything more to do with it when she saw the look on his face.

"Sean, that would be stupid, we have no idea what could be in there," said the older child trying to sound mad, but failing to hide the look of unease on his face from his mother. Something about the pile was making his mother scared to be close to it and that made him nervous. He hastily put his jacket on and looked at his mother.

"No, Hun, we're not going to dig in the dirt today," Mary began, "We don't have time for it. Your grandparents are going to be at the house this afternoon and Momma needs to clean."

"Okay, Momma," Sean said with all traces of disappointment gone when he heard his grandparents were going to be visiting.

"Well, we better get moving," Mary said as she ushered her children away from the mysterious mound.

The wind began blowing again and Joey zipped up his jacket

as he walked. Mary pulled out a scarf and wrapped it around her neck to keep the bitter bite of the wind away from her skin. Sean skipped along happily, occasionally glancing back in the direction of the mound.

Mary reached down and held her boys hands as they headed back home. Neither she nor Joey noticed Sean waving behind them to the old, scraggly bearded man that had crested the small rise next to the rock pile.

"Oh Lord, thy will be done," panted the old man, his thick Cajun accent even more muffled as he walked up the small hill with his arms full of rocks. Sweat rolled off his beard and eyebrows in a constant stream and he could feel a hard pressure in his back, a dull ache that seemed to have gotten worse with every step he took.

He felt a moment of panic as he saw the woman and two kids walking away from his newest cairn. He nearly dropped his load until he saw the smallest boy look back at him, smile and then wave. For a brief moment the old man felt more peace than he had in the past year, even the pain in his back subsided. The child was the first person to acknowledge his presence since he had started his journey. The old man smiled and nodded toward the boy.

When the family was out of sight, he carefully placed a layer of rocks around the top edge of the cairn; he then found two large sticks that were roughly the same size as each other. He pulled out his knife and cut off enough of his beard to tie the small branches together.

After the sticks were tied he pulled out a carefully folded cloth from his front right pants pocket. This was the part that he hated the most, he knew he couldn't look in the cloth even though he knew he had to have been the one to place whatever item it contained in its folds.

He knew he couldn't look, and he knew he would never remember what it was. That was just the way it had been for this past year, ever since he had gotten what he called "The Thing."

It was "The Thing" that had compelled him to leave his family in New Orleans and travel up the banks of the Mississippi River, and to places beyond, to build these damn rock piles. It was also "The Thing" that kept him from remembering what he was putting in them.

He placed the folded cloth on the cross section of the sticks and began filling the area in with dirt and rocks. Once he had the mound completed to his liking he slowly set off to the north, following the banks of the river as he had done for so many months.

"Oh Lord, when you gonna' let 'ole Abi go on home?" He drawled over and over again wearily.

He tried to whistle, but his mouth was too dry to make any notes. He felt parched, actually more thirsty than he could ever remember being before in his life.

His feet carried him close to the edge of the water and a strange calm came over him. He knelt down next to the river and saw his haggard reflection staring back at him from the muddy river.

He watched in fascination as his image became less weathered and started smiling at him, all the while seeming to get younger. The muddiness of the water slowly faded away and he could see himself wearing robes so white they almost shone with their own light.

He suddenly felt as though the weight of one the cairns was on his chest and he couldn't breathe. He felt himself falling forward and the cold waters of the river covering him up. He felt the waters dragging him down into darkness. A darkness that was suddenly driven away by the most beautiful light he had ever seen.

It would be two weeks before the body of Adolphe Billadeau, Abi to his friends and family, would be found in the Mississippi River just north of New Orleans. His family would hold a small funeral service for him, closed casket of course due to the decay and bloating of the body.

Those that knew him could only shake their heads in confusion and would never understand what had caused such a devoutly religious man to abandon them a year ago without a word of explanation.

If you asked anyone at the factory they would tell you Doug Tyler had always been a man that wasn't afraid of hard work. He would pull a double shift without batting an eye and would happily take any overtime that was offered.

He liked his job, it more than provided for his family, but the sad fact of the matter was that Doug Tyler didn't like his family very much. He would never admit it of course, just like he would never admit the reason he took all the extra shifts was so that he could stay away from them.

When he worked a half day on Saturday, he would stop in at one of the bars in town before heading home. Doug and a few coworkers would normally enjoy some drinks and then go their separate ways. Today was different. Today, he was drinking alone.

Doug heard some news earlier in the day about Charlie Miller, a former classmate, who had just signed a deal to work for a major news company as a foreign correspondent. Doug's dream had always been to work in the news and when Mary ended up pregnant...

Doug slammed his glass down on the counter of the bar and motioned for the bartender, Derek, to fill it again.

"Slow down man," Derek said as he poured another gin and tonic, "Mary is going to kick your ass if you come home drunk again."

"Fuck Mary!" Doug hissed as he took the glass from Derek.

"Whoa man," Derek said, "I didn't know things were bad at home. I was just jokin' aroun'."

"I ain't mad at you, I'm mad at... At just shit!" Doug downed his drink and wiped his mouth with his sleeve. "My life could've been something. I could've been something."

Derek looked at Doug for a few seconds before he responded, "You are something. You're a husband and a father. Man, that has got to be the best thing in the world."

Doug snorted, "Yeah, it's fucking great! Family keeping me in this shithole of a' town, wife always bitching I ain't never spending enough time with them. Real paradise, man."

Doug motioned for Derek to fill his glass again and the barkeep took the container and placed it behind the counter, "I think you've had enough for today. Why don't you go on home, Doug?"

Doug looked at Derek and glanced at the liquors on the shelf behind him. He licked his lips as he slowly stood up and pulled out his wallet. He took a twenty dollar bill out and tossed it on the counter angrily, "Keep the change, fucker! It's the last dollar I'm gonna' ever spend in this shithole again! Won't give me booze? I'll hit another fuckin' dive!"

Derek took the money and put it in the cash register as Doug left his bar. He watched him walk away and didn't see him staggering too much. He thought briefly about how mad Doug seemed to be and chalked it up as everyone having a bad day now and again.

Derek tended to the other customers and, after a little while, all thoughts of Doug and his troubles were completely out of his mind. He would most likely be back in next week and Derek would have a talk with him then about his attitude.

Derek went about his job as if everything was right in the world.

"Gampy!" Sean squealed as soon as the old man came through the door.

Bradley Knox barely had time to brace himself before he was suddenly dealing with all the energetic love a six year old could throw at him. As he picked his grandson up he held him at arms length and eyed the boy with mock seriousness.

"Think you can just hug me any time you want, huh?" said Bradley as he tossed the boy on the couch in front of him, "Well, take that!"

Sean giggled and laughed as his grandfather began tickling him. He tried countering the tickles with a few kicks and was making some progress with defending himself when his grandmother came in the door.

"Bradley!" She yelled, "What on God's good Earth do you think you are doing? The doctor told you to take it easy!"

Bradley stopped his assault long enough to glare at his wife, "Katie, if I can't play with my grandkids than what the hell good is it to keep on livin'?" He then proceeded about his task with renewed vigor, Sean laughing all the while.

Katie rolled her eyes as she took off her coat, "You stubborn ass. Let's just wait and see what your daughter has to say to you."

"And what am I going to say?" came Mary's voice from the top of the staircase.

Looking up towards the sound of her voice, Bradley saw the picture of Jesus he had given her as a housewarming gift. He was so proud when Katie and he had sold the house to her and Doug. He was just as proud now when he saw the picture prominently displayed above the second floor landing. His baby girl came around the corner with a smile on her face and rushed down the stairs to hug him.

"Dad, Mom, it's great to see you! How's life in Florida treating you?"

Bradley was about to speak but was interrupted by his wife, "It's beautiful down there. I was just telling your father that this summer you need to bring the kids down there for a visit. They would just love the beaches and we could all go sailing."

"Can we go, Momma'?" asked Sean.

Mary hugged her mother as she answered, "I don't know, Hun. We'll have to see if Daddy wants to go."

At the mention of her husband, Mary's mother stiffened in her embrace.

"He doesn't have to come along if he doesn't want to, Mare," she said, using Mary's childhood nickname.

"Of course he does, he's my husband," laughed Mary.

"He might be, but he, you know… He just doesn't act like it all the time," Katie said.

"What's Gamma' mean, Momma?" asked Sean.

"Go tell your brother to hurry up in the shower," Mary told

Sean, her eyes never leaving her mother's face.

"But what does…"

"I said go!" shouted Mary.

Sean was so startled he jumped. His eyes started to tear up as he ran up the stairs calling his brothers name.

"Katie, there was no call for that!" Bradley scolded his wife, "What happened back then is back then… Now is now."

"Mom, why did you even bring that up?"

Katie looked at the two of them and her stern gaze slowly faded, "I'm sorry, I don't know what came over me."

"Mom, maybe you would like some tea. I have some in the icebox if you want to grab a glass."

"I'd like that. I'll get it myself," said Katie as she walked into the kitchen.

Mary moved close to her father and whispered, "It's getting worse isn't it?"

Bradley looked at his daughter and nodded his head, "I think this will be the last time we can visit when she will recognize everyone."

Mary felt a pang of sadness. Her mother had been diagnosed with the early stages of Alzheimer's about a year ago. The disease was steadily getting worse and she was prone to bouts of meanness. During these fits she would say the most hurtful things for no particular reason.

Her dad had warned her that her mother was turning into a completely different person and he was having trouble dealing with it. He had also hinted around that it would most likely be only a matter of time before his beloved Katie would have to be placed in an assisted living complex.

The whole reason behind moving to Florida in the first place was to find a nice retirement facility. One that would allow the couple to stay together while she was able to get the fulltime care she needed from professionals. Bradley had a dark suspicion that eventually she would get to a point where she would become violent. If that happened, there would be no way they could stay together.

"I am so sorry, Daddy," Mary said as she hugged her father, "You know I am here for anything that I can do to help."

Upstairs they could hear the sound of a door being slammed

and some muffled conversation between the two boys.

"I know that, Mare," he said as he returned the hug, "But you know there isn't much a young woman can do. Especially when she is so busy raising two growing boys."

They held on to each other for a few moments, finally able to share a moment with someone else who fully understood the pain they felt in their hearts concerning the troubles that were ahead.

Their hug was interrupted by a smiling Joey rushing down the stairs. His short, damp hair sticking up in places on his head gave Bradley the impression of a hedgehog that was half angry.

"Grampa!" the boy said as he pushed himself between his mother and Bradley.

"Heya' Joseph!"

The old man tried picking up his grandson and gave up after a brief moment. The boy had gotten so big since he had last seen him! Bradley stepped back and visually compared the boy's height against his mother.

"Wow, you are so big now! You are almost as tall as your mother!" the old man said.

Joey beamed proudly then asked, "Where's Grandma?"

"She's getting a dri—" began Mary when she was interrupted by a loud scream from the kitchen and the crashing of breaking glass.

After his outburst, Doug had felt a little ashamed. Derek had always treated him good and he didn't deserve the kind of attitude that Doug had laid on him. *I'll apologize Monday after work*, he thought as he pulled into the parking lot of another bar he had been to a few times.

Doug knew that Derek was right, he should just go on home, but he didn't feel like dealing with hearing Mary bitch about him drinking again. He had promised her a few months earlier he wouldn't drink anymore, a promise that was made as a direct result of a violent outburst by him.

He had been out late one Friday after work, drinking with some of his friends. When he realized he was too drunk to drive, he had called a cab to take him home. While waiting on the taxi, he had a few more shots and one last beer.

He had been very drunk when he had gotten to the house. Mary met him at the door, demanding to know what the hell he was doing out so late. Doug couldn't remember the entire argument that followed, so he could never say for sure what had caused him to hit her.

All he knew was that when he had hit her, he had blackened her eye and it had felt good to do it. It was like all the years of frustration had come out in one rapid movement of his muscles. He wasn't proud of what happened, but he certainly didn't truly regret it either.

Doug shook away the memory, turned his car off and headed into the bar. Inside there was country playing, not his favorite music, but the singer was wailing something about lost dreams that caught his attention.

He stayed in the bar drinking and, with every sip he took, he became more sullen. The bartender finally had to threaten to call the police when Doug started verbally lashing out at the other patrons. Doug left in a tirade of foul language and with the promise to never lower himself to drink in such a rat-hole establishment again.

Driving home he ran a few stop signs that he didn't notice and he clipped the rear end of another vehicle that was parked up the block from where he lived. He stopped for just the briefest of moments and then, when he was fairly sure that no one had seen him, he drove around the corner.

He pulled his car into the alley behind his house, hoping he would be able to sneak inside without his wife or kids noticing he was home. If he could have seen himself through the eyes of any onlookers, especially the one whose car he had hit and was dialing 911, he would have laughed at the futility of his actions.

He thought he was moving with cat-like grace, but instead his movements were awkward and he stumbled more than walked. More than once he had to stop and use the fence as a makeshift crutch to keep from falling over.

He stopped halfway to the back door and looked around at his yard. The kids had left their bikes against the inside of the fence instead of putting them in the garage again. There was also a scattered assortment of other toys on the lawn, toys he could only vaguely remember getting them.

"Damn kids don't respec' nuttin'," he mumbled as continued his drunken surveillance of the backyard.

He worked his way to the door and fished around in his pockets for the keys, when he couldn't find them he pulled out his hunting knife and began fiddling with the lock.

He was actually surprised when the door opened and it took him a bit of time to recover from the sudden swing of fortune. He walked in the house and decided to grab a quick bite of food before sneaking upstairs.

He turned around the corner to go into his kitchen when a loud, wailing scream erupt right in front of him. He felt something hit him on the head and he instinctively lashed out with his arm to protect himself.

He felt just a small amount of resistance on the blade of the knife he was still holding and then something warm and sticky splashed on his face and arm. He tried focusing on the scene before him, but through whatever was burning his eyes and what had hit him on the head, it was hard to concentrate. He heard a strange sound, as if one of his kids was sliding across the floor, but then another sound made him snap to attention.

"Katie!" he heard a familiar male voice scream from the direction of the living room.

Doug turned to face the new sound when his vision cleared just enough for him to recognize his mother-in-law lying on the floor. Her eyes were open wide with terror and she was feebly trying to stop the flow of blood that was pouring from her neck. For some reason the image struck him as funny.

Something inside of him snapped. All the weight of his worries, his failures and the thought of everyone doing better than him suddenly hit him all at once. He knew, on some level of rational thought, that laughing was wrong in this situation. No matter how hard he tried though, he couldn't stop smiling as he looked down at the old bitch. Years of frustration came out in the form of a kick to her head as his father-in-law ran screaming into the kitchen.

Katie felt bad about the things she had said, even as she realized it wasn't really her fault. She knew she was sick and that there was nothing that could be done for her. Oh how she wished the disease wouldn't make her so mean sometimes!

She was taking her time in the kitchen and had already enjoyed a few sips of her tea. She was trying to calm down enough to go back in the living room when she heard a rustling at the backdoor.

I left the cat outside again, she thought to herself, *Why do I keep doing that?*

Katie stood up and headed towards the backdoor of her house. She saw a man come through the door with a knife in his hand and her heart froze. She backed away slowly a few steps as her mind raced for something to do.

When the man suddenly stumbled in front of her all she could do was scream and hit him in the head with the heavy glass mug that held her iced tea. She thought she actually might have knocked him senseless when his head first dropped low and his knees buckled. She had taken a step toward him, thinking she could push him over and call the cops, when he lashed out at her with the knife.

For just the briefest of moments she thought the man had missed her, until she tried to scream again and nothing came out but a wet gurgle. That's when the searing pain in her throat began. She reached up to check the wound when she felt blood saturating her blouse. She felt thick fluid pumping through her hand as she tried to stop the bleeding.

She slid against the countertop, her polyester clothing creating an eerie low screeching sound, until she was stretched out on the floor. She stared up at the intruder and was surprised to see that it was Doug. Only it didn't really look like Doug. His eyes were so hollow looking and he seemed to be staring right through her. The thing that terrified her most about him was the deranged smile he had on his face.

She heard Bradley yell for her and she tried again to yell out, this time a warning, but again the only sound that she could make was a gurgle. She started coughing and realized that her lungs were filling up with fluid. In horror she understood that she was choking on her own blood.

The pain in her neck started to subside a little, and sounds seemed to be coming from far away. She felt something warm running down her legs and hoped she hadn't peed herself. Doug continued to stare at her with that crazy smile of his until the door to the living room flew open and Bradley came running in.

She smiled up at her husband and then she knew only darkness when her son-in-law snapped her neck with one quick and forceful kick to the side of her head.

Bradley couldn't believe his eyes when he entered the kitchen, the scene before him was too surreal to even begin processing. His beloved Katie, wife and companion for forty-five years, was lying in a fast spreading pool of blood and his son-in-law was holding a bloody knife and smiling at him.

"No!" the old man yelled as Doug kicked Katie in the head, as casually as if he were getting a piece of garbage away from his shoe.

Bradley charged at Doug and swung a right cross with all the force his rage could summon. He missed as the younger man ducked under the blow and came up with the point of the knife leading the way into his stomach.

The old man let out a gasp of air as he felt his legs go numb and fall out from underneath him. He realized he was being held up by Doug and the damn knife that was sticking in his gut. He let out a scream when Doug twisted the knife and began to saw back and forth while pulling up on the weapon, the smile never leaving his face.

Bradley's arms lost all strength and he swooned momentarily, when he regained his senses he realized he was on the floor next to his wife. He didn't know how he had gotten there or how he had managed to move his arms, but now they were busy holding in his entrails. The smell of feces and urine was all around him and he started gagging. He looked at the blood stained face of his wife and couldn't fight the tears that started to flow as he stared into her lifeless eyes.

"Run, Mare!" he tried to scream but the words came out barely above a whisper, "Get the kids and run!"

Doug stepped over his legs and entered the living room, roughly pulling his foot away from some of Bradley's insides it had gotten tangled with. Bradley heard Mary and Joey scream and then the sound of footsteps running up the stairs and someone beating on the front door.

The old man still couldn't feel his legs and he wondered if Bradley had severed some nerves in his spine when he first stuck him. More screams came from upstairs and the beating on the front door turned into a crashing sound. He tried to crawl towards the living room but he just didn't have the strength to move any more.

He was getting weaker by the second and he knew he was dying, he knew that as surely as he had known anything in his life. His thoughts drifted to Mary when she was a baby and when he and Katie had first brought her home from the hospital.

His mind played out a few more memories, the happiest ones in his life, and his vision slowly faded. He fought it for as long as he could and when he saw his wife looking down at him with a sad smile on her beautiful young face, he knew he couldn't fight anymore.

"Take me home, Katie," he whispered.

The image of his wife bent down and lovingly stroked his face. When she gently kissed him on his forehead all the pain suddenly vanished and he only knew joy.

Mary had no idea what was going on in the kitchen, but she was even more terrified when she heard her father's scream. Joey had grabbed her arm and was shaking and she had begun to subconsciously rub the back of his head. When the door opened and Doug stepped out they both started to breathe a sigh of relief, until they saw all the blood on him and the twisted smile on his face.

"Oh God!" Mary screamed as she pushed Joey in front of her towards the stairs.

Her son made a strange gurgling sound but ran as fast as he could. As the pair neared the bottom of the staircase there was a loud banging on the door, the sudden sound causing Mary's heart to leap even higher in her chest. Without looking she bolted up the stairs, all the while pushing her son in front of her and listening to the strange sound Joey was making.

Doug was right behind her and struck out at her twice, once slashing the back of his wife's neck. If she felt his strike connect she gave no indication of it and continued her sprint up the stairs.

Doug had heard the banging and he was surprised to see, through one of the small side windows on the front door as he ran past, two policemen standing on his front porch. It looked like one had just recovered from a kick and the next one was lining up to try to break the door down.

I don't have a lot of time, Doug thought as he ran up the stairs after his wife and eldest child, *They ruined my life. They need to pay!*

Mary was at the top of the stairs and turned just long enough to throw down a small end table at him, the one his mother had left him after she had died. Doug's anger was doubled when the cheap wooden table flew over his head and he heard it smash against the wall.

"Daddy, stop!" wailed Joey, "We'll be good!"

Mary had moved in front of the boy, who had fallen and seamed to be frozen with fear. She was waving her arms in front of her, as if making the motion for him to go away would work. The cut on her neck had caused blood to spread over the shoulders of her shirt, the sight of it made Doug smile wider.

He stepped forward and slashed at her, cutting her on the inside of her right arm. She gasped in pain and then continued screaming. There was a loud cracking sound from the front door and the sound of glass shattering.

"Police!" yelled a new voice echoing up the stairs.

Doug snarled like a wild animal and grabbed his wife by the top of her hair. She screamed even louder when he pulled her closer to him and stabbed upward with his knife, ripping into her flesh just below her left lung.

"No!" Joey yelled and flung himself up from the floor towards his dad.

Doug yanked the knife out of Mary's tender skin while pushing her to the ground away from him. Joey made it a few steps before his father hit him in the temple with the handle of his knife, using a backhand strike. The young boy crumpled over the side of the staircase and made a sickening *thud* when he landed on the hardwood floor below.

"Joey!" Mary wailed.

She started crawling down the staircase, her eyes focused on her oldest son lying on his back and moaning. She noticed that the side window on the door had been busted out and a crack was across the center of it. Through the now glassless window she saw a police officer pointing a gun.

A loud explosion ripped through the living room as the officer shot his gun at Doug. The deranged man felt something zip by his head as he bent down to plunge the knife into Mary's back.

She moaned a few times, but continued to crawl down the stairs towards her wounded son. Doug was relentless with his strikes and she felt each plunge of the knife as it entered her body. There would be a small numbness until the blade was pulled free and stuck back in.

She was staring at her son when the blade of the knife pierced her in the back of the head. The last image her living mind would ever hold was that of Joey staring vacantly up at her.

There was another loud explosion as the officer fired his weapon again. This time the shot hit Doug in his left shoulder and it spun him around. He was a few steps from the top of the stairs and the picture of Jesus was staring down at him. In Doug's mind, he was already judging his soul.

He was so intent on the image of Christ that he almost overlooked his youngest son, who had been showering while the horrible massacre was taking place, staring down at him.

Doug reached out and grabbed Sean, who offered no resistance, and pulled him close. He turned his son around and placed the knife on the boy's neck. He had just started to put pressure on the blade when the officer fired his gun again.

Sean didn't know what was happening; he had heard all the screaming and hid in the bathroom. When he heard the gunshots he came out and saw blood all over the hallway. He walked over to check on his father and froze when he saw his mother lying still with blood still oozing from cuts on her back.

His father grabbed him and turned him around. It seemed he was being turned very slowly and then he felt the knife at his throat. He wasn't so much scared as he was thankful he wasn't looking his dad in the eyes anymore. His father wasn't in there, it was something else. Something that was dark and evil.

His father suddenly let him go when another loud bang echoed up from downstairs, although the knife did cut him very deeply from his shoulder down his right arm. He felt something warm and wet all over him and he saw blood and other pieces of flesh land on the picture of Jesus.

He watched as the blood dripped from the painting and mingled with that of his and his mother's. He slowly looked behind him and saw that his father had fallen in such a way that the stair railing was holding him up. Half of his father's head was missing and his right eye was bulging out of its socket.

The horrific scene would haunt his nights for many years to come. Blood and brain matter dripped from the gory wound while snot and spittle ran down his father's entire face.

The most disturbing thing about it was the smile on his father's face. He looked happier than Sean could ever remember seeing him.

"The wind shall eat up all thy pastors, and thy lovers shall go into captivity: surely then shalt thou be ashamed and confounded for all thy wickedness."

- Jeremiah 22:22

2

MAY BREAK MY BONES

Albuquerque, New Mexico – Four Years Ago

The priest leaned back and stretched his six foot frame as best he could in the confined space. He ran his right hand over his forehead, brushing back some of his light blonde hair that had fallen across his field of vision. Most people considered him an attractive and athletic man, although he was more wiry than muscled.

Father Thomas Murray had been taking confession for nearly fourteen years and during that time he had heard all manner of sins being committed. During those years it seemed that everyone had committed just about every sin possible at least once in their life.

Father Murray liked confession. It was his favorite part of the job, his favorite part of a job that had become all too boring and tedious for him as of late. Everyday had turned into the same thing. Sure the people were different, but they all had the same problems, and it seemed the more he tried to be active in their spiritual lives the less he actually ended up caring.

Confession, on the other hand, was exciting. It was when he learned that everyone had a side to them they wanted to keep secret. Some members of his church even seemed to enjoy telling him their sins, as if they were excited they finally had an audience for their exploits. It was like the parable of the Pharisee and the Tax Collector come to life.

Today was particularly slow however, and he found himself yawning more than was normal. The parade of old people coming in and confessing such ridiculous things as taking the last cup of coffee from their spouse or stealing their neighbor's paper just didn't even register on his list of things to be concerned about.

He was half asleep when the next member of his flock sat down in the confessional. The sound of the window slot sliding open startled him out of his brooding. The young woman, Laurie Alvarez, who had sat down was one of his favorite people to hear confession from and he smiled a bit as he leaned forward.

"Bless me, Father, for I have sinned. My last confession was two weeks ago," began Laurie in her low sexy voice, "In that time I have had impure thoughts of a man who is not my husband."

Father Murray was disappointed; Laurie was twenty years old and had been married just a little under a year. During that time she had cheated on her husband, who was in the military and stationed overseas, with more than nine different men and now to just hear she was having impure thoughts made him let out a small sigh. He had been hoping she would elaborate on an encounter like she did last time.

"My child, this sin is normal in those your age and in your situation," he said, "In this world, conflict often takes our loved ones far from us."

"Do you want to know who it is, Father?" she asked as she leaned closer to the window and dropped her voice low, "Do you want to know who I have been fantasizing about at night when I'm all alone?"

Father Murray's mind reeled. He licked his lips as his mind

raced for some response to the question she had asked him. He found himself staring through the window slot and he felt his face flush.

Father Murray had seen her in a bikini earlier in the week when she was doing a charity car wash. He could understand why men were attracted to her. Her long, blonde hair and bright blue eyes certainly caught his attention and when you looked at her body it was not hard to imagine what she looked like under those skimpy clothes.

"I'm so tired of confessing, Father," she whispered lustily, "Wouldn't it be easier for both of us if you already knew what my sins were?"

"Wha… What are you saying?" the priest said as he felt himself becoming aroused.

"I think you know exactly what I'm saying," the young woman whispered, "I know you look at me during services. I know you stare at my body, and I know what you want."

Father Murray silently cursed himself. He had been watching her a bit too closely over the past several months, her and a few other members. Last week when he had given her communion, he fantasized his manhood was in her mouth instead of the holy sacrament.

"This is a house of God. These thoughts and feelings have no place here!" Father Murray said, trying to sound angry but failing to keep the lust out of his voice.

"Oh, so you think we should take this conversation over to my house?" she playfully asked, "Or do you want to head into your chambers so you can properly give me my absolution?"

Thomas sat dumbfounded in the confessional, feeling his face flush and his lust building. There was no doubt in his mind that he wanted this woman, no doubt that he wanted to feel all the pleasure she could give him. He thought of his vows and of his future with the church, but they suddenly paled next to the intense physical feelings he was having.

He knew that it wasn't love, from what he had seen and heard from her he doubted Laurie was even capable of that emotion, and he knew there was a very real chance he would get caught. All of those thoughts only heightened his arousal and when he heard Laurie lightly panting through the window slot he knew what she was doing.

"So tell me, Father," she lowly moaned, "Do I have to keep doing this myself or are you going to help me?"

There was no defense he could muster against the urges coursing through his body. He could try to blame his weakness on the boredom that had become such a part of his daily life, or he could blame the brazen harlot that was pleasuring herself only a few short feet away from him. All in all, it boiled down to one thing; Father Thomas Murray had lost his faith years ago and had just been going through the motions.

"Come to my chambers, child," he said in a low guttural voice, "There is much atoning you need to do."

Laurie had gone home a few hours ago and Thomas was still feeling the effects from their afternoon encounter. The young woman was certainly everything he had imagined her to be. Her enthusiasm and skill was something he could not describe. She had kept him occupied for the better part of three hours and there was no place in his office that they hadn't used.

He could still smell her on him and his head swam with euphoria as he remembered parts of their lovemaking... No, not lovemaking... It was animalistic fornication. The need to take, use, release, and repeat had been all consuming to him.

He was roused from his musings when there was a rap on his door. He groaned as he stood up and walked toward the door in slow jerky movements, he felt like he had just hit every machine in the gym. He tucked in his shirt before opening the door and was greeted by Sister Anna Clair.

She wore her habit with dignified grace and waited patiently to be addressed. She once might have been a beautiful woman; however, her age was certainly a detriment now to her looks. Her grey eyebrows rested on top of eyes that might once have been soft, but over the years the taint of disappoint crept in and made them look hawkish and shrewd. Her aroma reminded him of the old leather bound books in his library.

"Yes, Sister?" Father Murray said.

"Father, forgive my intrusion on your meditations," the old nun's voice sounding gravelly with the strains of time, "There's a man here to see you. He said it is important and that it could not wait."

"Who is it?" asked the priest.

"It's Ryan Higgons," Sister Anna said with a faint smile on her face.

Father Murray felt a swift twinge of panic flow through him and grip him in the stomach. Ryan Higgons had been Laurie's most recent affair before him. Ryan had confessed the sin to Thomas and also had made it clear he wanted Laurie to leave her husband and marry him.

"How does he look? How is he acting?" Thomas couldn't help asking.

"He looks to have many worries, Father," she replied, "He is acting like a man who needs guidance."

The panic in Thomas slowly began spreading to his chest. If Sister Anna knew anymore than she was letting on she hid it well. The old nun had seen many things in her life and he doubted he was the first priest to ever have sex in these chambers. Father Murray had the sudden urge to shake the old woman until she spilled everything to him. He had to know what was going through her head.

"Is there anything else, Sister?" he asked with a slight hint of anger in his voice.

"No, Father," she replied with the smile still on her face.

"Then send him in," he commanded then shut his door.

Sister Anna gave a nod to the closed door and returned to the receiving area where Ryan waited. The old nun had indeed heard Thomas and the harlot engaging in their appetites. She didn't care much about the young lady, but she was very disappointed in the priest. As she entered the waiting room she felt a momentary twinge of pity for the young man seated in one of the many red velvety chairs.

The man was just a little younger than Father Murray, more physically fit and a few inches taller. He had black hair that was disheveled and his brown eyes were red from crying and seemed hollow to her. Sister Anna had overheard some of the distasteful discussions this man had with the harlot and hardened her heart as his attention focused on her.

He stood up when she entered the room and stuffed his hands deep into his pants pockets. Sister Anna noted his shoes and pants were dirty, as if he just came from his landscaping job.

"Father Murray is in his chambers. He said you may enter." After delivering the message, the old nun returned to the kitchen to finish her cleaning duties.

Ryan walked down the hall to Father Murray's door. He had been here a few times over the past three years for advice on important matters in his life. Today, he would be asking questions he never thought he would need to.

When Ryan knocked on the door he heard movement from inside. After a short wait the door opened and in front of him stood Father Murray. He was dressed in his robes and motioned him to come in with a smile on his face.

"Ryan, it's good to see you," Thomas said trying to sound cheerful, "What can I do for you?"

Ryan entered the room and sat down on one of the plush chairs in front of Thomas's desk. His hands were still in his pockets and he stared vacantly ahead. The priest locked the door then walked around his desk and sat in his chair. Ryan looked at him for few seconds and then began to cry.

Thomas was at a loss for words. If it had been any other member of his congregation, or if he hadn't indulged in his earlier activities, he would have walked around and hugged the man. As it was, Father Murray was feeling very uneasy in his presence.

"Father, I need your help," sobbed Ryan.

"What is it, my son? I am here for… The church is here for anything you need," Thomas corrected himself.

"It's Laurie, Father," Ryan continued to sob, "She… She told me earlier she didn't want to see me anymore."

Father Murray leaned back in his chair. So Laurie had broken it off with him. Thomas thought about the implications of that. Did it mean that he now had her full attention? The thought made him uneasy and excited at the same time. Looking at Ryan, he suddenly felt disgusted with the man.

Why was he crying his eyes out over a woman he never

should have become involved with, let alone attached to, in the first place? Ryan surely should have known that the situation was not going to end in his favor.

"Ryan, Laurie is a married woman. She made sacred vows to her husband, vows that you were directly involved in breaking with her," Thomas felt like a hypocrite when he first started speaking, but then the feeling changed over to one of superiority.

"Who are you to cry when it is you who have caused such heartache to come to that family? How do you justify your feelings when you know there never should have been anything between you at all? It's not love you're feeling, it is guilt!"

Ryan sobbed even harder as Thomas spoke harshly to him. He was hurting enough as it was and to hear the truth being spoken so coldly, as well as the unspoken truth, caused even more pain to stab through his heart.

"Father," he blubbered, "I have done something horrible!"

The next round of verbal bashing died in Father Murray's throat before he could utter it. He felt a chill run down his spine and settle in his toes. He looked at Ryan and clamped his mouth shut. The man was staring at him through his tears and his jaw was set with determination. Thomas slowly started pushing his chair away from the desk that separated him and Ryan.

"Father," began Ryan as he fought against his emotions for control of his voice, "I thought you were a good man; a man that was dedicated to helping others weaker than him; a man who understood that some things were sacred."

Ryan's voice became clearer and gained strength as he spoke. The tears, though still slowly and steadily falling from his eyes, started to draw less attention from Father Murray. Now, Thomas was overtaken completely by the emotion pouring from Ryan's soul.

"I know it was wrong," Ryan suddenly roared from the chair. His eyes narrowing as he stared at the priest who had fallen back into his chair at the outburst.

"It was all wrong, but I loved her! I loved her so much!" Ryan wailed as he jumped to his feet and leaned toward Thomas.

The priest slowly stood up and took a deep breath. Ryan

had started to drool during his tirade and the saliva was mixing with snot that had been hanging from his chin from all the weeping. Looking at the disgusting concoction made Thomas's stomach feel sick, a feeling that was pale compared to the fear that was rising sharply in him.

"Did you love her, too?!" Ryan demanded of the stunned priest.

"I... I... What do you mean 'DID' I love her'?" stammered the priest.

Ryan's growing fury exploded in the form of a left cross that connected squarely with the priest's jaw.

Thomas didn't see the punch that knocked him over the arm of chair. One moment he was on his feet and the next he was looking up at Ryan from the floor behind his desk. His nose crushed and splayed under his left eye.

"Unnnnhhhhh!" Father Murray groaned in shock as he tried to bring himself to a sitting position.

He could see Ryan slowly walking around the desk toward him through eyes that were fast watering up. He tried getting to his feet but was dizzy from the blow. Blood was flowing from his ruined nose and soaking into his clothes; he could taste more of it in his mouth and felt it in the back of his throat.

"Did you love her!?" Ryan screamed as he drug the priest to his feet by the front of his robe.

The sudden movements made Thomas feel faint and he felt like he was going to throw up. Ryan was gripping him so tight his skin was being pinched underneath his robe and shirt. Father Murray blinked several times trying to clear his vision and he felt a wave of nausea and then a moment of embarrassment when he vomited on the front of Ryan's shirt. Ryan seemed not to notice.

Ryan smelled blood on the man in front of him. The look in the priest's eyes was one of terror. The smells and look reminded him of what happened earlier and Ryan started shaking Father Murray like a ragdoll. Ryan also started wailing like a child who had dropped his favorite toy just out of reach.

Thomas's senses were reeling. His eyes were clearing up but his legs felt like rubber. If it wasn't for the painful way Ryan was holding him up, he realized he would have already fallen over again. When the crazed man started shaking him, more things came into focus.

"Leh' me go!" the priest screamed through his pain, his speech slurred.

Ryan gave no indication he heard Thomas, if indeed he had heard him at all, and continued to shake him. Thomas brought his knee up as hard as he could into his assailant's groin.

Ryan grunted and shoved Father Murray as hard as he could against the desk. The priest hit his back hard against it and twisted painfully over the heavy oak, comically landing in his chair for a brief moment before his momentum carried him over and onto the floor again.

"She was just a fuck to you!" the priest heard Ryan growl.

There was a deep burning pain in his back as Thomas got to his feet. His legs were still a bit shaky but he had them under control. He wasn't surprised to see that Ryan had moved between him and the door. He was surprised to see that Ryan was holding the silver letter opener that he kept on his desk.

"What do you want from me?!" screamed Thomas.

Ryan's face lost all sense of any composure as tears started rolling from his eyes again. His whole body seemed to convulse with sobs, and he kept wiping his eyes with his sleeve while making low moaning sounds like a wounded animal, never losing his stare on the priest.

"She told me about you," the shaking man said. "She told me she was fucking you and that she didn't want me anymore. She said she was tired of me."

Father Murray froze. Even though he had already figured out the reason for the attack he couldn't actually believe that Laurie had been so stupid! What kind of perverted thrill did she get from telling this psychotic a story like that? It didn't make any sense to Thomas.

"I told her I forgave her and that I would try to be more of what she wanted," Ryan said.

The priest watched as the man tried to regain control of himself. Each time it seemed he was getting close, another shaking fit would hit Ryan and the movements bordered on a seizure.

"Do you know what she did?" the man said between clattering teeth, "She laughed at me!"

Ryan made a lunge at Thomas, the letter opener leading the way. Father Murray shuffled to his left and leaned slightly back, the edge of the opener skipped across his ribs and he felt a brief flash of pain. Ryan's movement carried him in front of Father Murray and the priest made a wild swing at the larger man with his right arm.

By some miracle the blow connected and Ryan went down to one knee. Thomas swung a left hook and caught him just under the jaw. Ryan was knocked to the ground and the priest bolted for the door.

He was fumbling with the deadbolt when Ryan grabbed his head from behind and slammed his face into the door. More pain than he ever thought possible screamed at him from his nose and he felt himself being hurled to the ground.

He got to his knees just in time to catch Ryan's boot on the side of his head. He fell backwards from the force of the blow and stared numbly up at the ceiling trying to force his arms and legs to obey his will.

"I didn't know what to do!" wailed Ryan, his voice sounding very far away.

"She just kept laughing at me and I just wanted her to stop. I just wanted her to listen to me. I just wanted to explain how much she meant to me, and I would do anything for her!"

Father Murray saw Ryan above him and tried to roll away. He was helped along in that endeavor by a series of kicks from the crazed man. With each strike the priest felt more strength leaving his body.

"When I hit her she stopped laughing," Ryan whispered suddenly, stopping his flurry of kicks.

Thomas tried to understand the implications of what Ryan was saying, but the pain and fear in him made it hard. The priest rolled over onto his hands and knees and was startled to see the amount of blood that was falling from him. *No wonder I feel so damn weak,* he thought. Ryan's voice brought his attention back to what was happening.

"She started to scream so I hit her again. I kept hitting her until she was quiet. When I saw her like that… When I saw what I did… She was, just all quiet you know? She was so quiet but she kept staring at me. Blood was everywhere. She had stopped moving and laughing and she was just so quiet and so still. So quiet and still. She just kept staring at me you know?"

Father Murray dared a glance up at his attacker. Ryan had his back to him and was looking out the window. Outside there was flashing red and blue lights and Thomas felt immense relief flood through him. Sister Anna must have called the police when she heard the screaming.

Thomas tried to get to his feet, but he was too weak from the fight and loss of blood. Ryan must have heard him moving because he looked down at him. Thomas felt his arms give out and he collapsed on the carpet face down.

They both heard a pounding on the door a few moments later. Thomas started crawling toward the sound as best he could. He looked up at Ryan, who was just staring down at him with tears streaming down his face.

"I killed her, Father!" Ryan wailed, "I loved her, but I killed her!"

"Open the door! Police!" shouts came from out in the hall as the pounding on the door grew louder.

"I'm…" began Thomas, "I'm so sorry for all of this."

Father Murray continued to crawl toward the door. Ryan slowly walked alongside him, switching the letter opener from hand to hand. Thomas knew the man was going to kill him, he just didn't know when Ryan would work up to it. He did know that it would take a while before the police could get through the heavy oaken door with the deadbolt.

Thomas gathered all of his remaining strength and swung his right foot toward the back of Ryan's legs. When his foot landed just behind Ryan's left leg, the man tumbled down on top of him.

In a flurry of punches and shoves the letter opener somehow found its way into Father Murray's grasp blade first. Thomas felt the edge cut deep into his hand while at the same time he felt Ryan's meaty fist strike him in the back of the head and his vision instantly became blurry.

He got his left hand around the handle and began slashing wildly at Ryan. He managed to get into a sitting position while he slashed back and forth. Occasionally he would feel the blade of the opener hit Ryan, sometimes stabbing but most of the time cutting into his attacker.

All the while he could hear voices yelling out in the hall and then a much louder banging on the door, like a sledgehammer hitting it. The blurry form of Ryan was laying a few feet from him and was softly moaning. Father Murray stabbed him a few more times and each blow was met with a soft wet gurgling sound.

Thomas felt the opener slip from his hand. He no longer had the strength to grip it. He fell to the carpet meaning to just rest for a little bit. He could feel himself losing consciousness but held on until the police busted through the door.

Father Thomas Murray was taken to the hospital with several lacerations, a bruised kidney, a broken nose, four broken ribs and detached retinas. Ryan Higgons died en route to the medical facility from the multiple stab wounds he received during the fight.

The body of Laurie Alvarez was found in her apartment later that evening by police. When Father Murray was interviewed about the attack, he told police that Ryan had came to him for advice after committing the murder. Thomas lied and told police that he was attacked when he tried to convince Ryan to give himself up.

Sister Anna told police that Ryan Higgons had visited Father Murray on several occasions when he had a spiritual crisis and always seemed much better after talking to the Father. She also told police that she had called them because she thought someone was breaking into the church because of all the loud noises.

Thomas didn't know how much truth was in Sister Anna's story, but by the way she would always smile smugly at him when they were alone, he had a good idea of how much she really knew.

Three months later he requested and was granted a transfer from his superiors. Sister Anna smiled as he got into his cab and rode away from the church for the last time. She thought he was being transferred to some little town in Missouri, but didn't care much. She was just happy he was gone.

CHiLDREN OF ENOCH

"But I say unto you, Love your enemies, bless them that curse you, do good to them that hate you, and pray for them who despitefully use you, and persecute you; that you may be children of your Father in heaven. He causes his sun to rise on the evil and the good, and sends rain on the righteous and the unrighteous."

- Matthew 5:44-45

THE HORN ON THE BUS GOES...

Owensville, Missouri – Two Years Ago

Sean gazed through the window of the minivan and let out a small sigh, his breath causing the cold glass to fog up. He was happy that Miss Fritte offered him the front seat, even though it meant riding next to an asshole.

He looked over at the pudgy older man who was driving and then quickly wiped the fog away before Mister Dabner noticed what he was doing. Sean dared a glance at the backseat and felt a little better when Miss Fritte gave him a wink and a knowing smile. Sean returned the smile for a moment and then faced toward the window again.

"How much longer will the drive be?" he asked, not looking away from the scenery as it rolled passed.

Jake Dabner glanced in the rearview mirror long enough to make eye contact with Judy Fritte. The younger woman shook her head and had a worried look on her face. Jake made a snorting sound then looked back at the road.

"You don't sound too excited," said the kindly woman.

"That's because I'm not."

"Not a good attitude to have," Judy playfully scolded.

"Jesus f'in' Christ, Sean," Jake chimed in, "Do you have any idea how much work Miss Fritte has put in trying to place your sorry ass!?"

"Jake, don't start!" Judy snapped, "Things have been rough for him!"

"Oh hell Judy, things have been rough on everybody!" barked Jake.

Sean stared out the window as the argument got louder. He watched as the world sped past him, remembering similar trips in the past. Sean put his head against the cool window and felt the jostle of each bump on the road; it was very relaxing and made him tired. He closed his eyes and secretly hoped that this trip would be different.

"…don't you think, Sean?" Judy's use of his name snapped him back from the edge of sleep.

"Uh-huh," the boy said while yawning, not having any clue what he had just agreed with.

"I hope so because I'm getting tired of hauling you back and forth all the time," the fat man mumbled under his breath just loud enough for Sean to hear.

Sean ran his hands through his hair and stretched, ignoring Mister Dabner's taunt. It seemed like they had been driving for hours since they left the children's home in St. Louis.

"At least Owensville is a smaller town. They have almost no crime there," Miss Fritte said.

"Great that means everyone will know who the new orphan boy is."

He regretted the words as soon as he said them. He looked back at Miss Fritte and saw true care and compassion in her eyes for him. Sean knew the lady had tried everything she could to get him adopted the past six years and that she felt horrible that things always seemed to fall through at the last minute.

"I'm sorry, Miss Fritte," the boy said looking over his right shoulder at her, "I appreciate this, I really do."

"You better…" began Jake.

"You're welcome, Sean!" Judy interrupted, "I know you will do great here."

"I still don't understand what the Catholic Church is trying to prove here," Jake said towards Judy, "What kind of social experiment is this again? You take orphans from city facilities and place them in churches so they can be unpaid workers?"

"No, it's nothing like that!" she said, tired of trying to explain it to him.

"They live as a ward of the priest. They go to public school and can be as active in extracurricular activities as they want to be. They work ten hours a week as directed by their guardian and must attend all services."

"When participants in the program turn eighteen they can go to college and the church will cover all expenses for the first two years. After that it is based on their academics."

"What if I don't want to go to college?" asked Sean.

"In that case you'll need to find a job, kid!" Jake snapped at him.

Sean felt a moment of hate rise up in him towards the fat prick. He wanted to lash out, but instead he bit the inside of his lower lip and returned to staring out the window. His temper always got the better of him and was one of the biggest reasons he could never find a permanent home.

"You're a smart kid. You need to go to college," Judy admonished him.

The boy looked back at her and gave another brief smile, something seemed off about it but Judy thought it might just be his nerves. Making Sean smile was a mission for her daily. This morning since they had left, she had counted three of them, a new record.

St. Louis was far behind them and Sean was taking in all the open space along Highway 50. He had not been this far out in the country since that trip to a farm just outside of Washington. Sean had let himself forget the peaceful feeling he had while there, he knew peace never lasted.

"We're almost there, Judy," Mister Dabner said, "Damn this is a long ass drive!"

"Jake, language please!" scolded Miss Fritte.

"Awww hell, you have yer' head in the sand if ya' think these kids don't cuss," quipped Jake.

"Why can't you be nice to her!" Sean suddenly yelled, finally losing his temper.

The boy clenched his hands into fists and started banging on the dash of the vehicle. Mister Dabner glared at the boy and raised his arm as if to strike him. Sean stared back at him, daring the fat man to carry out his threat with the look he gave him.

"Stop it! Both of you!" yelled Judy.

"This little bastard needs to learn some respec'!" growled Jake, his eyes switching back and forth between the road and the child next to him.

"You need to learn it you fat fuck!" Sean yelled back at him.

Jake's eyes went wide and he gripped the steering wheel so tight his knuckles turned white. Sean continued to stare at Jake and each time the fat man looked over at him the boy's look became more hate filled.

Judy sat in the backseat feeling completely at a loss. She knew that Sean and Jake didn't like each other. Her stomach had actually turned when she saw that Mister Dabner was the assigned driver for the day. She had thought that there might be some kind of altercation, but didn't expect such venom.

She reached out and gently rubbed Sean's shoulder trying to calm him down. The boy was shaking with barely contained fury.

"Sean, try to let it go. There are people like him all over the world and you're going to have to learn to deal with them in a different way," she said.

"What are you say—" began Jake.

"She's saying you're a mean person that likes to hurt people. You're a bully, Jake, and I don't like you very much," Sean said.

The boy had come a long way over the years at getting his emotions under control and Judy could feel him stop shaking after he spoke. The calm and matter of fact tone in his voice was something to be commended. It was as if he was nonchalantly chatting about the sun outside.

"I think you—" Jake started.

"I think YOU need to just drive, Mister Dabner!" Judy interrupted, "There've already been complaints against you and I'll be making another when we get back. Don't say or do anything stupid for the rest of the trip and maybe mine won't be as bad as some I've read!"

Jake sputtered for a few seconds and then made some huffing noises. He kept his eyes focused on the road and the van was quiet for a few minutes before Sean spoke.

"I'm sorry, Miss Fritte. I didn't mean to upset you," the orphan said as he looked back at her.

"It's okay, buddy. Just try to remember that getting mad doesn't help anything. All it does is make it hard to think clearly. People do and say things they don't mean when they're mad," she replied.

The image of his father's death grin came to him and he shuddered. It wasn't hard for Sean to imagine how much anger and rage his dad felt. Sometimes, when he got mad, he just wanted everyone around him hurt. Even the good people like Miss Fritte.

After he had a chance to calm down he always felt bad about wanting that, but it never stopped the thought from entering his mind the next time he got pissed.

The sign for the junction of Highway 28 caught Sean's attention. He remembered Highway 28 had something to do with the town he was being taken to. As Sean was trying to remember, the van hit an uneven patch of asphalt and lurched to the left. Jake quickly recovered control of the vehicle and slowed down.

The fat man swore under his breath as he turned onto the new road and slowly built up speed. Miss Fritte leaned forward and gently put her hand on Sean's arm. The boy looked back at her and she squeezed his elbow, leaning in even closer so she could whisper.

"Don't let anyone like Jake Dabner make you feel like you're not important. Don't let them push you into doing something you'll regret later. People like that aren't worth it," she quietly said and then sat back in her seat.

Sean watched her retreat and then he looked over at Jake. It was almost as if he could see right into his heart. When Sean looked at him now, all he saw was someone who was scared and bitter about his own life.

Jake saw the boy eying him out of the corner of his vision and turned toward him with angry words on the tip of his tongue. He choked on them when he saw the look Sean had on his face. Pity was something Jake was not use to seeing.

Jake glared at the boy and mouthed "fuck you" to him. Sean turned away from him and watched the passing countryside again. After a few moments the orphan leaned his head against the window and let the motion of the vehicle carry him off to sleep.

Miss Fritte gently shook Sean as they pulled into the parking lot of the church in Owensville, Missouri. The boy stirred a bit but continued to sleep.

Mister Dabner turned off the van and looked at the bothersome kid seated next to him. A wicked grin flashed across the older man's face and he held down the horn for a few seconds.

Jake felt a rush of twisted pleasure as he watched Sean's eyes open wide with terror at the loud wail of the horn. The sadistic man chuckled when the boy started screaming and thrashing around.

"Damn it, Jake!" yelled Judy as she tried to calm the frightened child.

"It was only a joke, damn!" the fat man responded.

"You fucker!" yelled Sean.

"That's it kid, let the priest hear your potty mouth," laughed Jake.

The fat man kept laughing as Sean fought to regain his composure. Judy hugged the boy as hard as she could from the backseat. On instinct she reached down and held onto Sean's wrists, preventing him at the last second from lashing out physically at Jake.

Mister Dabner reached down and unbuckled his seatbelt while opening the door to the van. His laughter turned to a wheeze as he stepped out of the driver's seat onto the hard asphalt of the parking lot.

He looked inside through a side window as he stiffly shuffled to the back of the van. He rolled his eyes when he saw Judy whispering something into the kid's ear. Didn't she understand that the little freak was a hopeless case?

Jake leaned against the rear door of the van and pulled out a pack of cigarettes. Putting one in his mouth, he inhaled deeply as he lit it. He watched Judy continue hugging and talking to Sean for a few minutes while he smoked.

The fat man threw his half-finished cigarette down and ground it out under the toe of his right boot. He opened the back of the van and grabbed one of the kid's suitcases, grunting under the weight of it as he set it down next to him.

"Come on kid," he said as he reached for the next piece of luggage, "I'm not your personal fuckin' valet here. Move your ass!"

Sean flashed him a smile and slowly stepped out of the vehicle. Judy glared at him for a moment before opening her door and stepping out. Jake chuckled under his breath. Let the stupid bitch think filing a report would matter. He had too much dirt on the boss for him to get fired for anything short of murder.

Jake was about to yell at the kid again when he felt a firm hand on his right shoulder.

"Aww shit!" the fat man yelled. Jake jumped with fright and plunged headfirst into the back of the van.

He landed on his stomach and the wind was knocked from his lungs. Jake rolled over onto his back in a panic to see who had grabbed him. The sun hid the features of the figure standing in front of him. The fat man raised his arms up to try to block the glare and his heart beat faster when he felt two strong hands close over his wrists.

"Dem' words ain't nice ta' say," said a slow voice.

"I... I... Let me GO!" yelled Jake.

Sean and Judy came around to the back of the van and saw a heavily muscled middle-aged man in dirty grey overhauls holding Mister Dabner's arms. The man had a sad look on his boyish face as he looked down at his captive.

Jake kicked the man a few times. Judy winced in sympathetic pain as she saw two solid blows land in the stranger's crotch. The muscled man showed no reaction at all to Jake's struggles.

Sean watched in fascination as the man lifted Jake into a standing position. Sweat was pouring down the fat man's face from his struggles and his breathing was labored. It looked to Sean like Mister Dabner might have a heart attack at any moment.

"Apologize ta' da' boy and purdy lady," the stranger said slowly.

Jake stood dumfounded and stared into the man's bright blue eyes. His chest felt like it was on fire and he was gasping for air. He tried to pull his arms away several times and didn't so much as cause the strong man to even sway on his feet.

"Fer' da' words," the overhaul wearing man said, "Da' words ya' said ta' da' boy in front uh da' purdy lady."

Jake tried falling backwards into the van. He leaned back as best he could and tried to push with his legs. He was amazed as his three hundred and fifty four pound body was pulled back into an upright position by the stranger.

"Apologize... Fer' da' words."

Jake was at the end of his rope. He had never been man-handled like this before and he felt completely helpless. He started shaking from fear and fought back tears. The fat man tried to apologize but all that came out was a hacking sound and some sobbing noises.

Judy and Sean stood transfixed by the scene before them. Both of them had different thoughts in their minds. Judy, horrified at the thought of what might happen next, had grabbed Sean and was hugging him close to her. She feared that at any moment the large man would turn more violent.

Sean, on the other hand, silently willed the stranger to carry out Miss Fritte's unspoken fears. He wanted Jake's fat ass hurt, beaten and bleeding. Sean found himself smiling when he looked at the fear clearly painted on his tormentor's face.

"Michael, drop him!" commanded a new voice from behind them.

As soon as the last word was uttered the muscled man let Jake go. The fat man instantly fell heavily on his ass in the back of the van. Jake tried to stand but his legs were shaking so much from fear that it was impossible.

All heads turned to the man who had spoken. A young priest stood with his arms crossed in front of his chest and a sour expression on his face. A day's growth of beard was on the man's handsome face, giving him a rugged look that Judy found intriguing.

"He used bad words," Michael said slowly, "In front of da' purdy lady and da' boy."

"I know he did," said the priest. His expression softened as he spoke, "That will be all for today, Michael. I will see you tomorrow."

"K' Fadder'," Michael said, walking away like nothing had happened.

"Father Murray?" asked Judy.

"Yes and you must be Judy Fritte," the priest said as he walked over and shook her hand.

Mister Dabner had finally managed to stand up and was looking sheepishly at the group. Sean glanced at him and gave a cocky smile. The fat man did not have the energy to make any response.

"Please accept my apologies for Michael. He is a bit slower than most but there is a very kind heart in that huge chest of his."

"You could of fooled me!" grumbled Jake.

"Michael has… Strong opinions on how women and children should be treated. I don't think he would have seriously injured you, but it would have been best to just apologize for whatever you had done and not antagonized him further."

"Are you fucking serious?" asked Jake.

Thomas stared at him for a second before responding, "I think it best if you were to wait in the van."

"Fuck that!" yelled Jake, "I'm gonna' press charges against that fucking retard!"

Father Murray shook his head slowly back and forth then let out a sigh. "You must not be a fast learner my friend," he said while pointing in the direction Michael had walked.

As if on cue, Michael peaked around the corner of the church.

"Oh Fuck ME!" Mister Dabner yelled as he scurried into the

driver's seat through the rear of the van.

He cranked the ignition and when the engine started the fat man gunned the vehicle out of the parking lot, the back doors swinging wildly as he careened around a corner and sped up Main Street. Michael had watched him drive away and then disappeared around the side of the church again.

Sean laughed at the sight. He laughed until his sides hurt and tears were rolling down his cheeks. The boy laughed even louder when Miss Fritte joined in. Sean was wiping his arm across his face when he finally got a good look at the priest who he would be living with for the next six years.

Father Thomas Murray was looking at Miss Fritte with an odd expression. It reminded Sean of how some of the kids at the orphanage looked at potential parents when they came to visit. It was almost like a hunger.

Sean felt a chill run down his spine and he shuddered. When he looked back up he saw the priest looking at him. The odd, hungry look had been replaced with one of… Indifference?

"Young man, I am Father Thomas Murray." The priest said, "You can call me Father Murray."

"Yes, Father Murray."

"Don't sound so down," the priest said while smiling, "It can be a lot of fun around here."

Thomas looked at Miss Fritte as he finished his sentence then continued, "So should we call your boss and tell him you were stranded here or would you like to make other arrangements to get back home?"

Judy blushed under the gaze of the handsome priest and smiled back at him, "I guess other arrangements can be made."

She instantly felt like a fool. Flirting with a priest… What was she thinking? When she looked up at him to make some small talk her breath caught in her chest. Father Murray had looked her up and down a few times, and blatantly so! He must have wanted her to see him do it.

Judy felt her face flush and she was a little embarrassed. She looked at Sean. The boy was silently watching the exchange between them. Judy had learned long ago that Sean was a very bright child that picked up on subtlety a lot more instinctively than most adults. She briefly wondered what he was thinking, but stopped when the priest touched her arm.

"I have some business to take care of in Union tomorrow," he said while slowly moving his hand down her arm until he lightly held her hand in his, "It would be no trouble for me to drive a little further. Of course that would mean you would have to stay the night here."

Miss Fritte felt her face flush even more as she looked into Father Thomas's eyes. There was something in them, something mischievous and playful, which made her instantly attracted to the man.

Father Murray smiled gently at her and let go of her hand. He turned and lifted one of Sean's suitcases with far greater ease than Mister Dabner had managed. The boy looked at him for a moment then hurriedly picked up his remaining piece of luggage.

"If you both would care to follow me we can get things squared away for the evening," said the priest as he walked toward the church.

The orphan walked after the priest, the heavy suitcase causing him to sway awkwardly. Judy followed Sean, but her eyes did not leave the priest's body as she moved towards the church.

"I think you're gonna' like it here, Sean."

Sean glanced back at her and stopped himself from nodding when he noticed how intently she was looking at the priest. Sean felt a moment of jealousy wash over him, but quickly suppressed it before it turned into rage.

This guy was a priest. There was no way anything would happen between Miss Fritte and him! The orphan allowed a few moments of muffled laughter for himself before he followed Father Murray into the church.

Thomas lay on his back and watched Judy sleeping peacefully next to him. He allowed a smile to creep onto his face as he carefully got out of his bed and made his way to the bathroom. He thought about the evening's events as he relieved himself.

After showing the kid to his room, he had taken both of them out to dinner. Once back at his house next to the church, they had all watched *Star Wars* and then he and Judy put Sean to bed.

Seducing the lady had been easy after that. Yes, he thought him and the boy would get along great. Yes, he would look after him like he was his own. Yes, he always wanted kids, but being a priest…

Judy had been a very willing partner. Almost more so than the young foreign student he was currently involved with. Jacqueline was a sophomore at the University of Missouri in Rolla and she was anxious to experience all of America, including the decadence.

Father Murray lay back down next to her and looked at her naked body. He had a brief fantasy about introducing the two women to see where things would go, but quickly dismissed the idea. Most likely Miss Fritte would wake up and, once she was thinking more clearly, would hate herself for what happened earlier.

The fallen priest closed his eyes and slowly drifted off to sleep. His last conscious thoughts were of the uncomfortable drive he would have to make in the morning to take Judy back to St. Louis.

CHILDREN OF ENOCH

"Then the LORD God made a woman from the rib he had taken out of the man, and he brought her to the man. The man said, "This is now bone of my bones and flesh of my flesh; she shall be called 'woman, ' for she was taken out of man." For this reason a man will leave his father and mother and be united to his wife, and they will become one flesh."

- Genesis 2:22-24

4

GIVE THE DOG A BONE

Owensville, Missouri – One Year Ago

It might have been the steam that was making it uncomfortable, or it could have been the hundred or so sewing machines that were constantly running in the factory, creating a constant hum that would stay with the workers long after they left for the evening. Justin wasn't really sure which, all he knew was that it was hot and the fan he had set up near his desk wasn't doing much in the way of providing relief from the heat.

Even for July in Missouri it was hotter than normal, not that you could call any weather in the Show Me State normal. The heat combined with the sound of multiple needles whirring up and down made working conditions at Headwear, Inc. miserable.

The heat was more of an annoyance than anything else, as he could easily ignore all the noise in the baseball cap factory. Getting use to the weather was a lot tougher for him and he still had to wipe the sweat from his forehead and get the fog off of his glasses occasionally.

He'd started working in the company right after he graduated from high school, that action had surprised everyone that
knew him. Justin had a sharp mind and excelled in all his stud-
ies. He had even gone on to graduate third in his class, right
behind his cousins, Clay and Lisa.

By now most of his friends had either already graduated
from college, or spent time serving in the military. Justin had
thought seriously about going to a university but at the time
he just really wasn't sure what he wanted to do for the rest of
his life. As far as the armed forces, well, he was a realist about
that. He just didn't have the body for it, and knew he wouldn't
last a day in training.

Even now as the sweat poured down his face and stung his
eyes he wished he would have worked more on his physical
shape and less on his mental prowess. If he had, then maybe
the girls would have paid more attention to him.

Throughout school, Justin did make a lot of lady friends,
of course they were more interested in having him help them
with their homework than they were in dating him. All of them
gave the same excuses, "We're too good of friends", "You're
sweet, but I like so and so", "Can't we just be friends". Justin
had heard just about every reason and understood that they
were just trying to spare his feelings.

Still it would have been nice, if painful, to hear the real reason. Something like, "Justin, you're a great guy and I love
talking to you. You're charming, sweet, and you make me feel
good when I'm around you. But if I go out with you, people
will laugh at me; besides I don't find you attractive and you
need to lose weight." That kind of truth would have done him
a lot of good… after he got over the initial hurt.

The only thing, other than all his friends, that kept Justin
from feeling loneliness was his faith in God. When he was
younger he had found the acceptance he needed in the Church
of Christ and was overwhelmed by the amount of comfort he
felt in the presence of the Lord. He was also amazed at how
the comfort and feelings of love came faster and stronger the
more he prayed, no matter where he was or what was bothering him. Each day his trust in God grew and four years ago he
woke up knowing what he wanted to do with his life.

He started by doing charity work in St. Louis at a homeless shelter, spending the weekends feeding people and helping spread the word of God. During his vacation that year, he went to India and helped flood victims try to start their lives over. His spare time was filled with visiting the elderly at nursing homes. He enjoyed talking to those that had no one else to turn to, and during these visits he learned a great deal about how rural life was during the Depression and the World Wars.

He took classes over the internet, went to all the seminars that he could, and finally six months ago he became an ordained minister. That day was one of the happiest he had ever had in his life, but the best day by far was when he met Brenda three years ago on his birthday, a present from God himself.

Justin loved old Irish music and once in a while his friends would take him to O'Donnell's Pub, a bar in St. Louis that had live Irish bands every night. It was a Tuesday on his 25th birthday in December, and the crowd was a large one for a weekday. He ordered a Guinness and eased back into his chair, enjoying the house musician's rendition of *Johnson's Motorcar* when he saw her at the next table.

He wasn't exactly sure whether it was motion or something else that drew his gaze to her, but he firmly believed that God had his hand in it. What he saw stole his breath away. Brenda's eyes were the deepest green he'd ever seen. It was like looking into a field in the middle of spring and it echoed all the pictures of Ireland he had ever seen. Her hair reminded him not of fire but lava, deep red, and when she turned her head it rolled over her shoulders like waves.

Justin was pretty sure it was her eyes that took his heart, but he did have to admit that her hair had a lot to do with it. He had always wanted to see hair like that and was mesmerized.

He didn't know how long he had been staring at her, and probably would have continued to for the rest of the night if his friend Matt hadn't nudged him. Both tables got a good laugh at his expense and he went over to apologize to the green-eyed beauty. When he was standing next to her all he could stammer out was, "I'm sorry you're beautiful."

His words had run together, which brought on another round of laughs. She looked up at him, smiled and said," It's okay; I get apologies all the time for being beautiful."

Justin chuckled at that and offered to buy her a drink. After that they talked for awhile and made plans to meet the following Saturday back in the pub.

All the way home that night Justin tried to rationalize why such a lovely and athletic women would want to be seen in public with him. He thought that maybe it was because Matt would be coming along. His friend was the kind of man that Justin saw women drool over. He was handsome and had this easy-going expression on his face at all times. Women were constantly giving him their numbers and trying to make dates with him. Matt would take their numbers and then deposit them in the closest trashcan. His friend was happily married to one of the most beautiful and intelligent ladies Justin had ever had the pleasure of meeting.

The following Saturday night she gave Justin a hug when they met, then they spent the evening talking and dancing. Brenda only made the smallest of conversation with Matt, which made Justin feel better about himself than he had in years. At the end of the night, she invited him back to her place and he gladly accepted.

Once they got to her apartment, she kissed him, his first, and it was from an angel. The feelings that coursed through his body were unlike any he had ever known before. Their arms and hands started to wander over each other's bodies as they continued to kiss. When her hand went to his crotch he awoke as if from a dream. "No Brenda, please don't," he said.

He explained to her about his religious beliefs and told her that no matter how much he wanted her, he couldn't do that. She sat on the couch and didn't say a single word, she just sat there and stared at him. Justin apologized and hastily left. As he was driving home, he thanked God for giving him the strength to resist the temptation, but a small part of him was urging him to go back to her place.

Justin still felt the longing for her touch on him and thought that he would never see her again. His shock was complete when he got home and heard her voice on his answering machine.

The next day, she drove eighty miles to join him in church

and let Jesus into her heart. That day Justin not only had found the love he was looking for, but he also helped save a soul.

Today marked three years to the day, and they had been a couple ever since. Two years ago she moved out of her apartment in St. Louis and into his house in Bland, a small town of six hundred people located right off Highway 28 in the middle of Missouri.

All those memories came back to him as he sat at his desk, the useless fan just blowing steam from the irons into his face. For the third time that hour he reached down to feel the small box in his pocket, a reassurance that he still had the ring. It wasn't as nice as he had hoped it would be, but it was all he could afford. Besides it was a simple and humble little ring, just like Justin himself.

Today was the day he would ask Brenda to marry him. To be his wife and have his children. The thought of it brought so much joy into his heart that he didn't know if he was crying or if it was the steam.

The buzzer rang signaling the lunch hour. He had made arrangements two weeks earlier to leave at noon today so he could get the house ready. He still had to pick up the flowers at the florists and get them set up around the kitchen before Brenda got home at five. He had plenty of time to do everything he planned, but he didn't want to take any chances.

Justin stood up, turned off his fan, and gathered up a few odd and ends from his desk. He started to bend down to empty his trash when a voice drew him from his thoughts.

"Happy birthday, Justin! How's God doing today?" Without looking and even over the dying hiss of the irons he knew it was Craig.

Craig was a nice enough guy and could be described as having an average man's mentality when it came to sex. Always thinking about women and what he would like to do to them. The problem was that Craig was handsome and he knew how to use that. Craig also loved to joke with Justin about God and religion.

"God's fine Craig, in fact he wants me to invite you over to his house this Sunday," Justin said with a smile.

Craig laughed, "No can do buddy. I have a date with a hottie. We're going fishing out there on the Gasconade, drinkin' some beer, and if everything goes good she'll be using my pole by sundown!"

Justin shook his head and rolled his eyes. "One day you'll realize what's important in life. I hope it doesn't come too late for you."

"This is coming from a twenty eight year old that's only been with one woman? Man, how can you even counsel people and give advice on shit you don't know anything about?"

Craig raised his left eyebrow, a trick that Justin had yet to master. "And don't tell me that all the answers are in that book," Craig finished by pointing at the Bible in Justin's hand.

"All the answers are here," said Justin holding up his white leather bound copy. "You just have to have patience and faith. Eventually the solutions and answers come to you. Craig, God knows we all have our flaws and he accepts that. He loves us unconditionally and forgives us of our sins. All we have to do is ask for it. He's always there for us and hears all of our prayers."

Craig's smile faded a bit, "He might hear us, preacher man. Hell he might even care about us, but you know what? He's never answered my prayers. He's never given me what I've asked for."

Justin slowly shook his head and wiped the sweat off of his cheek, "You think that just because you didn't get what you wanted that he doesn't answer prayers? I'm glad God didn't give me half of what I asked for. If he had, then I never would have met Brenda. Listen to me Craig and listen good, some of the greatest blessings we will ever know come so disguised that we never see them for what they are, not even after we reap the benefits."

Justin had tucked his Bible away in his briefcase along with the other items from his desk as he was talking, when he looked back up Craig was walking away.

"Sorry man, it's lunch time and they don't give us enough minutes for a sermon too. See ya' next week buddy," yelled Craig over his shoulder as he headed for the break room.

"Lord, show him the way to you," Justin silently prayed as he lowered his head, "Let your love guide him on the path to happiness and salvation. In Jesus' name, Amen."

Even though Craig always pestered Justin about religion, he knew that he was a good man and would do anything for him if he asked. It bothered Justin that Craig's soul was certainly in dire jeopardy, and all he could do was keep letting him know that God did truly care but the rest was up to Craig himself.

Justin pulled his pants up a bit and toyed with the idea of stopping and buying a new belt. When he reached down to pick up his trashcan he heard a tearing sound and felt the breeze from the fan, cool now since the steam was off, blow up through the newly torn hole in his crotch. He chuckled to himself and decided he might as well pick up some new pants as well.

Walking out of the factory he acknowledged the farewells of his coworkers with a smile, a nod or a "See you next week and God bless" for his friends. When he was almost to the door Blanche stopped him.

Blanche was a lady in her late sixties, thin with gray hair and a sweet smile. Justin had known her all his life and would be forever in her debt. She was the one that convinced him when he was ten years old to go to church with her. She helped him with his understanding of the gospel when he was just a kid by explaining what all the archaic words meant. *Funny,* he thought as she was walking up to him, *now she comes to me for guidance. Praise you Jesus.*

Today Blanche was wearing her usual assortment of jewelry. A small silver cross, Celtic in design, that Justin had given her after he was baptized all those years ago, and her massive wedding ring. Worn on the same hand and from the same man she had been with for over fifty years. When he saw the ring his hands went again to his pocket, patting the box yet again.

"Hello there sweetie," he said as he hugged her, "Afraid I was running off forever?" When Justin withdrew from the embrace he noticed the look on her face and realized that something was bothering her.

"What's wrong, Blanche?" he asked, genuinely concerned.

"Oh honey," Blanche began with tears slowly coming to her eyes, "I wish I knew." She started to cry then. Not sobbing or sniffling, but the tears flowed freely from her eyes. Justin, completely at a loss, held her close to him again.

"It'll be okay, honey," he whispered as slowly he rubbed her shoulders, "Whatever it is will be okay. Hush now, hush. God will walk you through it, and I'm always here for you. It's okay." He continued to pat her shoulder as he waved away the small crowd that began to gather. Craig stayed a little longer than the others and gave Justin a worried look.

Justin smiled at him and said, "She'll be okay bud, finish your lunch." Craig nodded and slowly walked back to the break room.

"Okay Blanche, tell me what's wrong. " Justin said in his most soothing voice.

"Let's go outside honey," replied the older lady, "I want to see my flowers."

"Hey, we can jog around the block if you want to," Justin said smiling. He took her hand and gave it a small squeeze as he opened the door for her, bringing a ghost of a smile to her face as he did.

Outside the wind gently rolled over the grass and the modest flower garden the plant manger let Blanche maintain. The day was cloudy, providing some relief from the sun but made the day almost too muggy to bear. She sat down on the small oak bench, another gift from Justin, and leaned over to wipe an insect off of one of the roses.

"I need to water them before I leave tonight," Blanche said offhandedly. Justin only nodded his affirmative, happy to see her calmer and less confused. This little garden of hers surely was a comfort and blessing. Justin was pleased that he was able to talk Larry into setting this aside for her, and he was very touched when Larry paid for the brick and small stone water fountain out of his own pocket.

"I'm worried about you, Justin," said Blanche as she leaned back into her seat," I was just in there cleaning the bathroom and got the most awful kind of feeling."

Justin put his arms around her and smiled, "Blanche you don't have to worry about me. The Lord is my guide in everything. I've lived my life in service to him and if something bad does happen just remember that I go to paradise. With God at my side, there is nothing to be concerned about. Everything is his will, for whatever reason."

Blanche smiled back at him then gave him a small kiss on his forehead, "You're strong in the faith Justin, much stronger than I ever was. The only reason I went to church for the longest time was just for the socializing and gossip. It took an innocent little boy to really make me believe in God. Now that you're older, I've realized that you never needed me, I was the one that needed you." Blanche's eyes started to get misty as Justin continued to smile at her.

"You brought me closer to God than I ever could have been," She continued as she blinked away tears, "and you have no idea how much that means to me."

"Blanche," began Justin, "It was God that brought you closer to him not me. It was also your acceptance of his love and his word that started it. If I had any part at all, then it was because he wanted it to be so."

The old lady took his hands in hers and stared at him for a few seconds then softly said, "I just want you to be careful today Justin, that's all. I know something bad is a coming. I can't explain how I know it, I just do."

Justin saw two things when he looked in her eyes, things that bothered him. Fear and concern. Justin let his smile drop and said, "Blanche, I'll be fine. I'm strong enough and with the Lord's help I can overcome anything. With faith we can move mountains and I can guarantee you that no mountain is going to fall on me today."

Justin put his hand in his pocket and slowly drew out the little white box. He was nervous about showing it to Blanche, in fact he hadn't even shown his own mother yet. His hands shook a little as he flipped open the top and showed his old friend the small diamond. Her eyes widened and her mouth fell open just the smallest bit. She looked from the ring to Justin and then back again.

"You're going to ask her today? That's why you're getting out of here early. Oh honey I'm so happy for you!" She grabbed him around his neck and rocked back and forth for a few moments.

"Hey she hasn't said yes yet," protested Justin with a laugh, "but I think it's going to work out good."

"Of course she's going to say yes," said Blanche, "I'm just surprised it took you this long to ask her!"

"I wanted to have enough saved up for the wedding and the honeymoon. After payday I'll have enough set aside for both," said Justin with a wink.

"And where do you plan on taking your lovely young bride?"

Justin smiled again and looked at the grass dancing in the wind, "I want to go to Ireland, Dublin to be precise. From there we'll rent a car and stay a few weeks touring the countryside. You know, stay in roadside bed and breakfast houses. It should be a great time."

Blanche laughed, "Of course at night you'll be doing a different kind of sightseeing, right?"

Justin blushed and stammered, "Well I don't… I mean yeah I hope so, sure."

Blanche stood up and pinched his cheek, "You get home and propose to that girl. Call me tonight with all the details. Don't worry about what I said earlier, I suppose I just felt a big change coming on and took it the wrong way."

Justin got to his feet, "Yeah, I'm heading to the flower shop now to get three dozen roses. I'm going to put them all over the house, light some candles, and have dinner ready for her when she gets home."

"It'll still be daylight when she comes in, what are the candles for?"

"They're scented candles, strawberry in fact. She loves strawberries; I just thought it would be a little something she would like. Besides with my culinary skills, I need to do something to cover up the smell."

Blanche and Justin both chuckled then she said, "Well, good luck, but I don't think you need it. If you get occupied don't bother calling, I'll see you in the morning. You can tell me all about it then."

Justin opened the door for her and waved as she entered, he then got into his old Ford Crown Victoria. He heard his pants rip some more as he sat down and went over how much time he could spare shopping. It would take at least a half hour to get home, then maybe fifteen minutes at the florist.

Checking his watch and doing the math that would put him

back in Bland by one. He knew that if he went shopping he would spend at least forty-five minutes in the store. He just couldn't spare the time today, maybe after work on Friday he decided. He rolled down the window of his car and pulled out of the parking lot.

"Even as Sodom and Gomorrah, and the cities about them in like manner, giving themselves over to fornication, and going after strange flesh, are set forth for an example, suffering the vengeance of eternal fire."

- Jude 1:7

THIS OLD MAN CAME ROLLING HOME

Bland, Missouri – Later That Day

The drive from Owensville, the town where the factory was located, to Bland was only a fifteen minute drive. At noon in the summertime, however, it took that long just to get out of town. Teenagers, out of school and unemployed, zipped around in cars and trucks, just having fun and being young.

Most of the young ladies only wore bikini tops and it was hard for Justin not to at least cast an admiring glance their way. This was usually met with giggles, and one time he got flashed. He somehow managed to stay on the road, but he knew he must have been grinning like an idiot for at least an hour.

As Justin was turning up Main Street, a young lady in a blue Ford truck ran her stop sign and very nearly slammed into the side of his car. Justin stomped on the brake pedal and turned his wheel sharply to the right. He heard the screech of the trucks tires followed closely by its horn honking at him.

When Justin looked up the woman was yelling something unintelligible at him and was flipping him off. The only words he could clearly make out were "asshole" and "motherfucker". In response, Justin stuck his head out of the window and asked, "Are you okay, Ma'am?"

"No, I'm not!" the lady screamed, "You almost killed me you fat motherfucker!"

Justin considered for a brief moment about arguing that fact, but instead he drove up the block and took a side road back to Main Street. As he pulled onto the street he saw that the lady was still in the middle of the intersection and was out of her vehicle looking at the front end of the truck. Traffic had backed up two blocks and people were honking horns and yelling at her to move out of the way.

He quickly lost interest in the event and continued up the road to the stop light. After waiting a few minutes his light was green and he took a right onto Highway 28 and followed the traffic out of town. After leaving the city limits, he lit a cigarette, took a long drag, and slowly exhaled the smoke. Smoking was one of only two habits that Justin considered a vice. He had tried to quit on several different occasions but after two days he was tense and his temper got the better of him.

The last time he attempted to give up cigarettes he had made it three days and thought that he was in the clear. It was a Friday and he decided to celebrate by having a few beers with his friend Chris. They went to St. Louis and after a few drinks the urge to smoke was overpowering. Chris had laughed when Justin asked him for a smoke.

"I thought we were celebrating your new found freedom from addiction," Chris had said while he handed him the cigarette.

"Well now we can celebrate my return to the fold," Justin laughed back.

Justin had only half heartedly tried quitting since that night. It seemed that drinking, his other vice, made him want to smoke even worse. Although he was nowhere near what anyone would call an alcoholic, he did like to have a few drinks on Friday and Saturday nights.

Of course sometimes he would drink a little too much and Brenda would have to make sure he made it to bed. Those situations rarely came up, perhaps only twice in two years and only on Friday nights, but he knew they did happen and that it was one of his weaknesses.

Justin leaned back in his seat and enjoyed the drive. The window let a steady breeze in his vehicle and cooled him down well enough to be comfortable. It also was a reminder that his pants were ripped.

As Justin entered Bland he looked at his watch and gave a grunt. The small sidetrack in Owensville cost him and if he wanted to keep to his schedule he couldn't take the time to stop by his house and change pants. He sighed as he passed his street and continued toward Belle.

Bland, although rent and taxes were cheap, offered almost nothing in the way of services. Granted the town had a gas station and a small store where food could be purchased, but most other items needed to be bought out of town.

Belle was a good place for little odds and ends shopping. It wasn't much larger than Bland but it had several restaurants, stores, and a large supermarket. It was also only a five minute drive from his home and Justin honestly believed that the two towns would eventually be connected.

Most travelers through the area marveled at all the small towns grouped so close together. Although the communities themselves only had between 900 and 5,000 people, they were very different from each other. It had seemed that small town life had bred into itself a strong sense of xenophobia.

The old timers in the towns seemed proud of the fact that their towns had been pretty much the same for the past 50 years. Outsiders rarely asked for directions twice, for these usually came in the form of "What ya' gotta' do is go on down this road and turn right after you pass John Smith's place, you know 'ole John don't ya?" The area was certainly stuck in a mire of its own making.

As Justin entered Belle he thought again about all the missed opportunities he had by growing up in this town. The school had done its best to educate the kids, but working on a very limited budget made it almost impossible to prepare them for the real world.

He remembered one school board meeting argument that broke out when he was a freshman in high school. The board had approved the purchase of some new computers and some people were not happy about it. If computers were bought, then the agriculture class couldn't get a new welder. It seemed that some small-minded people didn't really understand what computers were; much less what they were capable of.

Justin turned onto a narrow road that led over the now unused railroad tracks. He couldn't remember the last time a train had rolled through the area. He thought the tracks were part of something called the Rock Island Line, but he wasn't positive and did not want to look like a fool for asking something like that.

As he went over the tracks the small bump caused his pants to tear just a little bit more. He checked to see how much of his crotch he had left. After a quick glance he determined that if he stood up with his legs closed nobody would be able to see. And he would have to walk a little bent over but he would be ok.

Luck was finally with him when he saw an open parking spot directly in front of the florist. He pulled in and shut off his car, but as he looked at the shop his stomach clenched a bit.

After all this time he was finally ready and almost prepared to go through with his proposal. He was so close to seeing the fruition of all of his hopes and dreams, and yet he was terrified.

His mind flashed through all of the things that could go wrong. In that one moment his head was spinning and he leaned on the steering wheel of his car for support, his hands gripping the dashboard. His eyes tried to take in his surroundings but he could find nothing to focus on. Justin found himself gasping for breath.

Am I having a heart attack? He thought offhandedly.

After a few moments he managed to get his breathing under control. He felt his heart rate returning to normal and he pushed himself away from the steering wheel. As he leaned back in the seat there was a loud knock on his driver's side car door.

Justin jumped in his seat and banged his head on the roof of the car. As he glanced over he saw one of the local police officers looking at him with a concerned look on his face.

"Holy crap, Justin, I'm sorry!" said the young officer as he opened the door, "Are you okay?"

It took Justin a moment to recognize the man as the most recent addition to the Belle police force. His mind flipped around a few names until it found one that seemed to fit.

"Frank?" Justin asked, putting just enough of a question in it so it wouldn't sound too offensive if he was wrong.

"Yes, Pastor Grady," Frank said as he extended his hand. "It's a pleasure to finally meet you. I've heard nothing but good things about you."

Justin smiled and took the offered hand and shook it warmly. As he released it he noticed that the officer seemed a little nervous. Justin slowly let the smile leave his face.

"What's wrong officer?" he asked. Then he thought about the incident in Owensville and he felt like he was going to vomit.

He didn't think he had hit the truck. He couldn't remember feeling a bump or being knocked around in his car. A mental picture flashed in his mind of the woman looking at her truck, and his stomach clenched again. He had heard stories of people blocking things out, and he silently began praying that his mind hadn't done that to him.

"Justin," the officer began, "were you involved in an altercation with a woman in Owensville about twenty minutes ago?"

"Yes, sir," Justin said, letting his voice trail off.

"Well, first thing is that there was no accident. You didn't come close to hitting that truck."

Justin visibly relaxed and took in a lungful of air, it was only then he realized he had been holding his breath.

"OPD has about six witnesses that say she ran a stop sign and came close to ramming into you. After you left she went to the police station and tried claiming you hit her truck." Frank allowed a smile to creep into his face. "That was her mistake."

Justin stared blankly at Frank, trying to figure out how a mistake could be made by going to the police.

"It turns out that the nice young lady was strung out on

meth," the officer replied to Justin's questioning expression. "It took OPD a little bit to figure out what was going on. She came in and threw a piece of paper with your license plate number written on it at the dispatcher. Then she started screaming and cussing. Once they got her restrained she told 'em you hit her truck and took off."

"How did they find out that I didn't hit her truck and that she was on drugs," Justin asked, "Did they check to see if fresh paint was on it?"

"It wasn't that scientific, Pastor Grady," Frank laughed, "While she was in the holding area a man came in and said that the driver of the truck in the police parking lot snorted some kind of powder before she got in it and drove off. He was coming in to report the entire incident and was grateful to see that she had went straight to the PD."

"Well that's good news!" Justin exclaimed as he shook his head. "I'm glad somebody decided to let the police know what they saw."

"Yeah, it was one of those 'Worlds Dumbest Criminals' moments that's for sure! The Owensville cops searched her truck and there was meth, pot, and a little coke," Frank said, "I just wanted to let you know the entire situation, Pastor Grady. This way you know for sure what happened and to keep an eye out for that crazy woman while you're in Owensville."

Frank extended his hand again and said, "It was a pleasure to meet you. Like I said I have heard nothing but good things about you, sir."

Justin shook hands with him and said, "Well, let me say thank you for everything you guys do and it would be a pleasure to see you at church on Sunday."

"I would, Pastor Grady, but I'm Catholic and Father Murray would ream me a new one if I jumped faiths." Frank smiled again, "You take care now and if you need anything just let us know."

With that Frank walked across the street to where he had parked his patrol car. Justin watched him as he got in and noticed he was talking on the radio with a smile on his face. He waved at him as he pulled away and Justin gladly returned it.

Justin barely managed to remember to keep his legs together as he got out of his car. As he closed his door a white mini van rolled slowly past as the driver waved at Justin. He recognized her from his church, and he waved back grinning.

When he entered the florist shop the various smells washed over him. He stood near the door for a moment letting everything sink in. He looked around at all the flower arrangements and even slid his hand over a nice bouquet of yellow and blue ones.

He had seen the type of flowers several times before, but didn't know the names of them. He could only easily recognize and name roses and dandelions.

He passed other items in the shop, vases, teddy bears, cards, and even some mirrors on his way to the desk. He rang the bell as he leaned on the counter and looked around for someone to help him.

He had called in his order last week and spoke to someone that sounded familiar to him, but he couldn't place the voice. The mystery was solved when a raven-haired woman came out of the door that led to the storage room.

Jodi Cox's family had moved to Belle from Owensville the summer after his eighth grade year. He was the first person she had met in her new school. Justin had loved her during their high school years. She was beautiful and haunted his dreams during that time. She made everything feel right in the world for him, as if nothing could ever go wrong in his life.

Sadly he learned that friendship was all he could get from her. He had asked her to go to prom with him and she had agreed to go, but only as friends. Justin was hurt, but he knew it was his only chance to hold her close.

The dance was magical. They had danced and sat with mutual friends, ate together, and at one point she had squeezed his leg. His hopes soared and he thought something must have happened to change her mind about him. When he took her home that new found hope was shattered.

Jodi gave Justin a hug and told him that she had made a date with Scott Branson at prom as a car pulled up to her house and honked it's horn. All Justin could do was watch her get into Scott's car and slowly drive away from his life.

He had heard that they got married and that she had twins just six months after the nuptials. Later on, Scott supposedly caught Jodi cheating on him and divorced her. Justin could hardly believe she would do that.

As he stood in front of her now he could see that life had taken its toll on her. Her eyes no longer held luster and her movements, once the most graceful thing Justin had ever seen, now suffered a stiff formality to her gait.

She smiled as she recognized him and even that seemed to have been forever altered. Watching her as she moved to the counter Justin realized the truth that had somehow managed to elude him until just then. Love really does make you see things differently in people.

"Oh my God!" Jodi squealed as she leaned over the counter to give him an awkward hug, "I was hoping I would still be here when you stopped by!"

Justin held her for a brief moment. He allowed himself to get lost in her smell and to feel her arms around him. He told himself it was time to let her go when he could feel her hot breath on his neck, but it was only after she started to pull away before he finally released her.

"It's been," Justin's words caught in his throat and he coughed to clear it," a long time, Jodi."

She stared at him and continued to smile as she said, "Yes it has been! The last time I talked to you was at graduation."

As she finished speaking Justin felt his face twitch. He remembered how he had walked away from her. How he had basically walked right out of her life. As he looked at her he wondered how much different his life might have been if he had stayed a part of hers.

He thought of Brenda and wasn't too surprised when he could see the similarities of appearance between the two. Really the only noticeable difference was in the color of the eyes and hair.

He smiled at Jodi then, most of the concerns of his past suddenly lifted from his soul. God had truly given Justin what he had asked for all those years ago, but in His divine grace had given Brenda the eyes and hair Justin was drawn to. It was finally time to lay some things to rest.

"About that," Justin began, "I really think I owe you an explanation for what happened."

Jodi crossed her left arm over her chest and tussled her hair with her right hand, something he remembered her doing whenever she was nervous. Once again he felt like he was back in High School, but this time he found that he had no difficulty talking about how he felt.

"You know I had the biggest crush on you," he said with a grin, "I knew I didn't really have a chance to be with you, but I couldn't help how I felt. You made me feel good about myself whenever I was with you. You listened to me and cared about me. That had never happened before with anyone."

"You were always easy to talk to Justin." She said, "That's one of the things I liked about you."

"If I seemed to have led you on back then I am so sorry. I didn't want you to feel like you weren't important to me." Jodi said as she looked down at the counter.

Justin looked at her and smiled before continuing, "I didn't know how to make myself stop the feelings that kept me awake at night, or the feelings that made me jump up and rush for the door each morning just wanting to see you. Everyday that you weren't in school seemed to last an eternity, and I kept hoping and praying that it wasn't anything serious and that I would see you the next day."

Jodi's hand stopped playing with her hair and slowly lowered itself until it rested on the counter next to Justin's. He looked in her eyes and for a moment he thought he could see the life coming back into them.

"You had to have known what I was feeling towards you. I couldn't hide it no matter how hard I tried, everyone else could see it too I'm sure. The thing was, I thought that eventually your feelings for me would change. Now that I'm older and a little wiser, I know that it was just adolescent day dreaming, but at the time Jodi... it was really the only thing that kept me going."

"When we went to Prom, well, it was the happiest day I had ever had in my life up to then. The happiest and the saddest day all at once and there was nothing I could do to stop it. After I watched you leave with Scott, all of my dreams left in that car with you. I felt so empty and dead inside, like there was no point in even trying anymore. If it wasn't for God, I am sure that I wouldn't be standing here now."

Justin had continued to hold her gaze as he spoke. The more he talked, the more free he felt. More and more of the burden was being lifted with each passing moment, and he regretted not being able to do this years ago.

"I did everything I could to avoid you for the last few weeks of school that we had left. When you finally left me with no way around it, I told you the only thing that I could at the time. I only hoped that you would be able to understand, or that at least one day you would."

Justin took a deep breath and felt his legs starting to feel shaky. He put his hand over Jodi's and gave it a small squeeze. She turned her palm over and returned the comfortable embrace.

"I am so sorry, Jodi," he lowered his head as he spoke. "I am so sorry I threw away our friendship. I was one of the most precious things I had ever known. I am sorry I wasn't stronger back then and, most of all, I am sorry I wasn't what you wanted."

Justin looked up at her as he finished talking, he could feel a small gathering of moisture at the corners of his eyes. It was the last of the closure he had needed for so long leaving him, and leading him closer to his new life.

He could see by her expression that she had known the reasons all along. He hoped that after all this there would be no more questions in her mind, no more wondering if there were any other reasons why he had walked away. He also hoped, against his will, that she would carry regret with her for what might have been between them.

"Justin," she said," Of course I knew how you felt about me, but something I could never tell you was…"

Her voice trailed off as she looked at him. Justin thought she was looking for the words, those magical little words that would bring her the comfort he believed she needed. When she spoke again it took him a little bit to register what she was telling him.

"I liked you," she said while staring at the counter. "I just was so worried about how people would act around me if we got together. I worried about my friends and what they would say about you and me. You're saying that you're sorry to me, and all along I should have been the one saying I'm sorry to you."

"My life hasn't been the greatest since school, Justin," she looked up at him and her voice started breaking. "I have made some really bad choices. Scott Branson was one of those choices."

"I was so worried about what other people thought that I didn't listen to my feelings when I should have. Even now looking back, I can't believe I was so stupid and superficial."

"I always hear people talking about what a wonderful man you are, about how you always help others with no thought of yourself. I hear some of the girls that use to make fun of you in school say how they wish that they could be with you."

Jodi squeezed his hand harder, it was only then that Justin realized that they were still holding hands. A part of him understood he was still trying to hold onto just a little bit of his past, for just a few more moments at least. Hold onto it until he was forced to walk away again.

"I've wasted too much time worrying about how other people see things Justin. I know that you have a fiancé, and you might think me terrible for saying this, but if things don't work out with her, please call me."

She turned abruptly and walked back into the storage room, leaving Justin with a jumble of emotions he thought he was finally over. He watched her as she walked away, and again her movements were beautiful to him.

He bowed his head and asked God why he was being tested on today of all days. He pictured Brenda's smile and the feel of her arms around him, and her lips on his. That was what he wanted now, more than anything, even in light of the revelations he just had from Jodi.

The sound of the storage door opening returned him to

the present, and seeing the three dozen Roses in Jodi's hands made him smile. How ironic it was to him that someone who used to hold his heart in her hands now held the flowers that were meant for someone else.

Jodi placed the flowers on the counter and hit some keys on the cash register. The door slid open and she shut it before Justin could even take out his wallet. He looked at her in confusion.

"It's the least I can do for you now, Justin," she whispered.

"Thank you, Jodi, for everything."

He picked up the flowers and started to turn around when she placed her hand on his shoulder and stopped him. As he turned back to the counter she was holding a small piece of torn paper out to him.

"I don't know if you can take this but I really wish you would."

Justin took the paper and started to ask her what it was, but he heard the door open to the store and stopped himself as another male customer hit the bell on the counter and gave Jodi a playful smile. He walked out of the florist and put the flowers in the back seat of his car.

When he was buckled in he looked at it. She had given him her phone number and a hastily scrawled note that said simply —*Please call me!*

He threw the number into an old fast food bag in the trash can of his car and shook his head as he drove out of town. As he drove away he thought about how wonderful his new life was going to be.

Justin pulled into his driveway and checked his watch, he still had plenty of time to get everything ready, and after all the sidetracks he had hit he was very grateful.

His house wasn't anything to impressive, two stories tall and a full basement. The blue paint on the wood siding was starting to peal in various places and his gutters leaked. He was glad Brenda had convinced him to build a small porch on the front of the house; it added a little character to the place.

Justin wasn't much of a wood worker and the actual building of it was done by his brother Dan, who was in fact a professional carpenter. The stairs were strong and sturdy and, most importantly, bore his weight without creaking when he walked on them.

His brother certainly did a fine job, even added a few additions that Justin and Brenda loved. Dan had included benches on both sides of the porch which were more comfortable than most of the chairs in Justin's house. He had also put on a roof to the porch that melded easily with the actual roof of his house and sloped up gracefully to connect with it.

Above the porch roof his brother included another mild surprise that really had pleased Brenda. In the area just under where an old window had been, was a small sun deck and a tinted sliding glass door for access. The area was just large enough for two chairs and a small table to set drinks on. Since that had been built last summer it was Justin's new favorite place to go and watch as the world moved past him. He and Brenda spent most every evening up on that little deck.

His brother had insisted on painting it white to offset the color of the house, and after he was done with that, he took it upon himself to paint all the shudders on Justin's house white to match the porch. The finished project would include stripping the old paint off the house and applying a new coat, which was the plan for the second weekend of August.

Justin closed his eyes and imagined how it would look once the painting was done. He was sure Brenda would be happy with it and that was the most important thing in the world to him. He also had an idea for a small gazebo to place in the flower garden in the back.

Brenda had claimed the small backyard as her own the minute she had moved in. His friend Matt's mom had always been a wonderful gardener and she and Brenda had made an instant connection.

Matt was happy with the situation as well. Since he had moved to California his mother had received less and less visitors. Even though Justin still stopped by to see how her and his dad was doing at least every couple of weeks, he knew that she must get lonely sometimes.

Matt's father had been a truck driver for as long as Justin had known the family and it kept him away from the house more and more it seemed. With Brenda as a visitor and traveling companion, a lot of that loneliness had been alleviated. During the summer it was not uncommon for Brenda to stay a few days over at their house to help out in the garden, or for Matt's mom to be seen napping in the spare room when Justin got home from work.

"You done really good finding that woman," Matt had told him once during one of his visits.

"Mom loves her to death and thinks she is the 'bees knees' as she puts it."

Justin couldn't find any grounds to disagree. They were always together and had so much in common. Once again, he was grateful that she was finding such acceptance amongst his closest friends.

Of course this summer was a little different. Brenda had started working at a small factory in Bland towards the end of October. Justin had been supportive of her decision to go back to work, even though he felt like he was a good enough provider. She had ended the argument before it even really began by saying that she felt like she needed to bring some extra money in now because when they decided to have kids she wouldn't have much time for anything else.

Justin stood on his porch for a moment and fumbled with his house keys. He moved as slowly as he could to avoid damaging the flowers, a silly notion really since he planned to take two dozen of them and scatter their petals all over the house, but he hadn't decided which bouquet to give to Brenda and didn't want to risk that being the one he messed up.

As he walked in the house he eased the door shut, another little project he had kept putting off. When the door was being closed you had to lift up on it a bit to get it to latch right, otherwise it would blow open if any breeze hit it.

Once the door was closed he set his keys on one of the small end tables by their couch and started to walk toward the kitchen to put the Roses in some water when a banging noise from upstairs caught his attention and he heard a man's voice.

Justin slowly walked to the stairs and cocked his right ear toward the sounds upstairs. There was more banging, the man's voice again, and other sounds he couldn't recognize.

Oh Lord we're being robbed! He thought. Justin looked around in a panic, trying to spot where the phone had been set down at. He spotted it on the charger and picked it up and hurriedly dialed 911.

After a few rings a ladies voice on the other end answered, "911 what is your emergency?"

Justin had started slowly walking up the stairs as he whispered, "My name is Justin Grady. I just got home from work and someone is upstairs in my house robbing me. Get someone here quick."

Justin held the phone tighter to his ear as he continued up the stairs, wincing at each creak of the steps. *I have got to fix those*, he thought absently as he continued his ascent.

"Sir, can you make it out of the house safely?" he heard the lady's voice say.

He was about to answer when he heard what sounded like someone stomping on the floor above him. He heard the man's voice again, but still couldn't make out what was being said. "Hold on," he heard himself say into the phone while another feeling started to come over him, it was of shear dread.

Justin continued to move slowly, feeling more and more like he was in a nightmare with each step. His legs felt like they were made of rubber and it took every ounce of his will to keep putting one in front of the other.

A voice came from what seemed like miles away, "Are you okay, sir?"

Justin looked down and noticed that he still held the phone in his hands. He also registered that he was clutching the roses to his chest and could feel some of the thorns poking him through his shirt.

He again heard the man's voice and also heard what sounded like grunts as he made it to the top of the stairs. He found himself standing outside Brenda's door with his hand on the knob. He pressed his ear against the door and heard more grunting and now a slapping sound. He also heard the voice much clearer.

"You like that?" it said. "You like it when I slap your ass while I'm fucking you?"

Justin's breath caught in his throat. *This is a dream wake up. This is a dream wake up. Oh God please let me wake up!* His thoughts screamed at him.

"Yeah smack it harder baby, smack my ass harder! Make me scream, I wanna' scream!" it was Brenda's voice that time, unmistakable even though Justin refused to believe it.

The slapping got louder and he heard Brenda moaning, whether it was from pleasure or pain he didn't know. His hand started to turn the handle on the door and a calm voice entered his head, a voice that was much too calm and soothing to be his own at this time.

Don't open the door, the voice begged. *Don't put yourself through more pain then you are in now.*

He ignored it. He had to see with his own eyes what was happening, even though the pain in his heart already told him it couldn't be anything but a hellish scene. His hand was still on the handle but refused to obey his command to turn the knob. From inside he heard more moaning and the sound of what could only be the bed bouncing on the floor.

"Oh, God, fuck me harder!" Brenda screamed.

As Brenda was yelling out her obscene demands the sounds of the bed shaking stopped, Justin almost breathed a sigh of relief but then they started again.

Justin heard a grunt coming from the man, and heard Brenda moan long and loud. It was then that he finally managed to open the door. Everything slowed around him, in his mind it took an hour for the door to swing wide. In those few moments he heard only the sound of his heart, he could feel the blood as it moved through his veins. He could feel it burning; could feel it freezing all at the same time.

The sun coming from the tinted sliding glass door didn't let a lot of light in, but his eyes saw more than enough of the room to understand what he was seeing. Brenda was on all fours on the bed; her back was arched up allowing him a clear view of what was dripping down her.

The man was stroking himself and was starting to turn toward the sound of the opening door. Justin recognized him vaguely, from church he thought. Justin then felt his hands being ripped, being shredded from something. He felt something warm running down his arms and he smelled something metallic.

Justin heard someone screaming, he didn't know if it was Brenda or the man with her. It might have been his own screams, he didn't know for sure. It was the most unnatural thing he had ever heard. He felt his throat go dry and he tasted blood in his mouth.

The world exploded red in front of him and his hands felt like they were on fire. He looked through the haze and felt nothing but hate at what he saw. Slowly the red began to fade, and as Justin blacked out the last thing he saw was a cascade of rose petals falling all around him and for a second he thought he felt gentle hands trying to pull him out of the room.

The scent of roses and blood followed him into the darkness.

Justin Grady would never be able to remember what happened that day after he blacked out and most people counted that as a blessing for him. The police report that was filed outlined some horrific actions on his part.

While responding to the 911 call, an officer spotted Brenda running from the home. She was naked and had blood spatter on her body from several angles. She was in hysterics and while the officer tried calming her down more police arrived at the residence.

Justin Grady had nearly beaten Jim Crouter to death by the time he was restrained. The wounds he inflicted would forever leave Jim with permanent movement loss to his right arm and mild brain damage.

One officer suffered a broken leg when Justin threw him down the stairs and the other cops finally had to use a TASER to get him handcuffed. The enormity of the emotional damage Justin was going through was evident in everyone who knew him, which was a lot of people.

Brenda moved in with her sister in St. Louis and Jim Crouter resided in a nursing facility for four months while he recovered. If Jim and Brenda ever spoke to each other after that nobody knows.

Justin Grady's bail was posted by his friend Matt's mother and father, using their home and land as collateral on the bond. The wheels of justice started their slow spin and Justin Grady, former pastor now turned alcoholic, was given a court date in late June of the following year.

"Make no friendship with a man given to anger, nor go with a wrathful man, lest you learn his ways and entangle yourself in a snare."

- Proverbs 22:24-25

BAA, BAA, BLACK SHEEP

Rosebud, Missouri – June, Present Day

The drive from St. Louis to Rosebud, the small town where his parents lived, was always enjoyable for Matt. The first thing he had done when he picked up the Jeep at the airport was to take the top off and roll down all the windows.

The weather, although not nearly as good as Los Angeles in Matt's opinion, was mild for June, and his plane had landed just as a storm had passed over. The afternoon still had the scent of rain in the air as he started on his way home.

Once he had driven passed Union, he slowed his pace to relax and take in the scenery. It had been almost a year since he had been home and he was noticing a lot of minor changes in the area. New construction vied for his attention against the winding road he was traveling.

While driving through the small town of Beaufort he was saddened to see that one of his favorite diners had changed its name, which most likely meant a change of ownership as well. Long ago and in what seemed like a different life to him, this was the place he had taken his high school prom date.

It was also from the payphone outside of the diner where he had called Justin to come pick him up at after he had drunk too much to drive. Looking over his shoulder he felt a wave of nostalgia sweep through him as he scanned the side of the building for that payphone, and he breathed a little easier when he saw it was still there.

No one understood why Matt, an attractive and popular guy in school, was friends with someone like Justin. It was something that Matt couldn't really even explain to himself. It was as if Justin was the balancing force that he needed in his life because they were certainly polar opposites in almost everything.

He had met him when they were both young, Matt was ten and Justin only eight, and there was just some weird connection that was made. He could still remember playing with *G.I. Joe* and *Star Wars* action figures with Justin behind his house on Pear Street in Owensville.

Matt also thought of all the conversations he and Justin had shared. Justin was always honest with him and would offer his opinion whenever asked for it. Unlike most people he didn't hold back, he was always tactful certainly, but he always let you knew where he stood on an issue. With Justin there was no illusion of who you were dealing with, there was no wondering what he might be planning or any thoughts of whether or not you could trust him.

Throughout the years as both Matt and Justin grew, both as adults and in their friendship, Matt knew that no matter what happened, Justin would always be there for him. That theory was proven correct on more than one occasion.

Matt couldn't even begin to count how many ways his friend had been there for him through the years. Thinking about it made him realize how much Justin had always been there for him when he needed him. Of course it was a door that swung both ways. While Matt drove along the winding highway he could think of two times Justin had asked him for help; two times that Matt had managed to betray his friendship.

The first was when they were barely teenagers and Justin had confided in Matt that he liked this girl in his new school. Matt finally convinced Justin to ask her out after already having his girlfriend, who attended the same school as Justin, talk to the girl first. Justin finally gave in to the pressure from Matt and asked her out on a date.

Matt had picked up Justin and his date then took them to the movies with him and his girlfriend. Matt still wasn't sure what exactly happened, but the night ended with Matt breaking up with his girlfriend and getting the number of Justin's date. He didn't tell Justin he got her phone number. He hadn't wanted to hurt him.

The good intentions he might have had in lying to his friend didn't help much. The small town in which they both lived was a mixed blessing and curse. It was only a matter of a few days before Justin heard the rumors that he was sleeping with the girl. Looking back, Matt knew that the relationship wouldn't go anywhere; he had just wanted to have sex with her.

As he drove along the mostly deserted highway, Matt wracked his brain to remember her name. He could still see her face and hear the small panting sounds she made as they had sex, but he couldn't recall her name. What he did remember in vivid detail was the look on Justin's face when he had asked him if the rumors were true.

It was an odd mixture of pain and acceptance, the look a man might have as he was marched off to the gallows in the Old West. Matt swore to Justin that he would dump the girl and that he would break up with her that very night, which he did. What he never told Justin, and hoped that he would never find out, was that he stayed the night with her that night anyway and several other nights the following year. After all, you don't have to be going out with someone to stick your cock in them. That was his second betrayal of the friendship.

Matt slapped the dash of his Jeep and swore in frustration. *What in the fuck was her name?* He kept asking himself. While passing a slow moving farm truck Matt decided that he would just call her 'That Girl'. It seemed very fitting actually. Most of the problems that ever bothered Justin could be narrowed down to 'That Girl', even if it wasn't the same one, just a different face and name. They had all treated his friend with the same attitude and intentions.

Justin was just too nice of a guy, laid back and caring. It was like every woman saw a sign above his head that said 'Easy to Use'. Where most of the men Matt hung out with were filled to the brim with testosterone and had an aura of confidence, Justin had the typical nice guy mentality and appearance. Always smiling a lot and cracking jokes, actually listening to those stupid bitch's problems and trying to help them out. He was forever stuck in the friend category.

Matt had tried to help Justin out with all the women problems that seemed to spring up. No matter how many times he had told his friend to stop being so nice to them it just never seemed to sink in. Any time a girl had a problem they would run to Justin to seek comfort or get advice.

Matt knew that his friend had a real soft heart and that he would get attached to them in one way or another. Unfortunately for Justin the only thing that they saw in him was friendship. This inevitably led to a few tears and long talks. The same conversations over and over again. All over 'That Girl'... All over him wanting more than any of them would ever give.

Looking back on all of them now, Matt felt nothing but contempt for the dozen or so women that came to mind. A few of their names he could easily recall: Lisa, Jodi, and Elizabeth; but for Matt it was easier to just lump them all together as people that used his friend.

As he drove along the ill-maintained highway he allowed himself to have a few moments of homesickness. As he entered the town of Gerald the feelings of nostalgia quickly changed to thankfulness towards the Marine Corps.

If it hadn't been for the service to his country he might very well have been trapped in this area like most everyone else he went to school with. It still boggled his mind how the people around here could be perfectly content with milking out a meager existence without wanting more out of life.

As he drove through the town he risked a glance at his uncle's house. True to what he expected, the place was in a sorry state of disrepair. He could remember a time when he and Justin had to throw his uncle Joe out of the house for beating up his aunt and twelve year old nephew.

Justin had originally tried to talk Joe into willingly leaving the house but when it became obvious to everyone that it wasn't going to work, Matt had grabbed the man and began wrestling with him. Justin helped him and they finally managed to get the old drunken bastard outside where they administered a country form of justice.

Even though his friend was a peaceful man by nature he never did let Matt down when it came to getting physical in a situation, but after it was all over with Justin always prayed for forgiveness.

That was something he never understood. If you stand up and did the right thing, why on Earth would you have to ask to be forgiven for doing something you had to do? It was only one of the many things about Justin that caused him no end of frustration over the years. Along with the frustration though, their friendship definitely had a lot of good times and laughter.

When Matt got to the city limits he gunned the engine on the Jeep and continued down the highway. He let all of the familiar sounds and smells of home wash over him and again felt some homesickness starting in the pit of his stomach.

He slowed down and forced himself to remember all of the reasons why he hated this area. The small minded bigoted people, the lack of decent education, the small town mentality of wanting to know everyone else's business, and the soul sucking feeling of being trapped.

While he was sorting out the jumble of emotions going through his mind he turned on the radio. The wailing and lamentations of some country singer assaulted his ears and he quickly changed the station. Too late for him though as the chorus replayed itself in his head, *"It's hell and high water... that you're going through, but come hell or high water... I'll be here waiting for you."*

He cursed at the person who had rented the Jeep before him. Matt could picture in his mind some fat assed good ole' boy wearing camouflage bib overhauls cruising around trying to pick up some of the local cows. The mental picture he had conjured up caused his temples to throb, a sure sign a headache was coming on, and he wished he had brought some aspirin with him.

After fumbling and cursing at the radio for a few moments he finally hit a station that was playing something a little more to his liking. He was having trouble hearing the lyrics but the song had a nice beat and a pleasant female voice was singing. Not wanting to press his luck out in the sticks he turned up the music instead of changing the station again.

His head started feeling a little better when he got into Rosebud. If Gerald was considered small town life, then Rosebud was something right out of *The Twilight Zone*. The town had not changed a bit since the last time he was here, which wasn't much of a surprise. Matt honestly believed that the town hadn't changed since the mid-50s.

The same buildings, the same kinds of people, and the same blatant disregard for traffic laws! As he was getting close to the only gas station/grocery store/bait shop in the town, a lady in a blue Mazda Miata darted out of their parking lot causing him to put both his feet on the brakes.

The screeching of his tires made him grit his teeth and his fingers to bite deeply into the steering wheel. If the other driver had continued moving there would not have been any problem but the woman driving, true to form or maybe because on some level she knew that it would just make his day, slammed on her brakes as well. When the two vehicles hit he felt himself jerked back and forth.

He sat in the Jeep and glared at the woman that was getting out of the car. For a moment he entertained the notion of what she would look like if he had been going faster, the thought was not an unpleasant one to him.

"I'm soooo sorry! Are you okay?" the lady was asking as she got out of her vehicle.

She was a pretty woman with short dark hair that came down to her chin and brown eyes. Matt admired the way her tight white shirt showed off her tits but suddenly felt a completely irrational anger towards her when he noticed she was wearing cowboy boots.

"What the hell!" he said making it an accusation instead of

a question.

"I didn't see you coming at all," the woman said, "You must have been flying through town!" she added accusingly.

Matt slowly unbuckled his seatbelt as the woman was talking and opened his door. Before he got out he retrieved his insurance information out of the glove compartment and put it in his back pocket.

"I was not flying," Matt began, "I was doing the speed limit. You drove right out in front of me and then, for some reason only a redneck-little-whore like yourself could comprehend, you hit your brakes." Matt kept his tone low, knowing if he started screaming at her he wouldn't stop.

"It's not like it would of taken you a lot of energy to actually look and see if anything was coming. I mean hell, it's not like you were pulling out onto a major roadway or anything, right?" Matt could feel his temples starting to throb even worse as he was talking.

The woman stared at him and he saw her jaw drop just a little bit. She stood there for a few seconds with a dazed and dumfounded expression on her face, which caused Matt to shake his head in frustration.

"Hello? Did you hear me or is everyone in this podunk-redneck town stupid and deaf?" Matt could hear his voice rising as he continued, "Why in the fuck were you in such a damned hurry anyway? Are they giving away free tickets to some jerk off singer with a mullet, or are you running late for your job at the strip club?"

"Fuck you!" the woman screamed at him and started rummaging through her purse.

"Don't worry sweetheart," he said as he pulled his cell phone out of his pocket, "I'll call the cops."

He dialed 911 as he went to the back of the Jeep to get a bottle of water out of one of his bags. He just got it opened when there was an answer on the other end of the line.

"911 what is you emergency," said a man's voice.

"My name is Matt Anderson and I was just involved in an accident on Highway 50 right in front of the Rosebud gas station," Matt said then took a drink of water.

"Are there any injuries?" asked the man's voice again.

"I'm all right and I think the ladies okay too," Matt said.

He turned around to see the woman was still looking through her purse. "They want to know if you're all rig—" he began to ask when the woman pulled a small can triumphantly out of her purse and pointed it at him.

It suddenly felt as if his eyes and face were on fire and he heard the woman scream, "Take that you cocksucker!"

That did NOT just fucking happen, he thought as he felt his eyes close and the membranes in his nose start to go crazy.

"How does that feel you arrogant cocksucker!" the woman screamed at him as he began flailing around from the effects of the pepper spray.

"You crazy bitch!" he screamed over and over again.

He was dimly aware that he had dropped his cell phone and he started scrambling around on the ground searching for it. The pain in his eyes seemed to be getting worse and snot was running out of his nose. It was starting to get hard to breathe and he was afraid he was going to pass out.

He could hear the 911 dispatcher calling for emergency personnel to respond to the scene. He forced himself to calm down as he crawled towards the sound. He could hear the operator asking him what was going on and he reached for the sound. His moment of calm quickly passed as he heard the sickening sound of a cowboy boot stomping on his phone.

"What the hell!" he screamed then he felt the point of a boot kick him in his lower ribs.

"Get the fuck away from me you crazy whore!" he yelled as he rolled away, fervently hoping he wasn't heading in the direction of the highway.

"Fuck you, you goddamned prick!" the woman shrieked at him.

For just a moment it got quiet, and Matt thought the lady had retreated to her car. That thought was shattered when he felt another sharp kick in his side. Off in the distance he heard the sounds of sirens.

"Fuck you!" the lady continued to scream at him, sometimes only a few inches from his face.

He did the only defensive thing he could think of, even though it wasn't manly or in anyway macho, he curled up in a ball and covered his head with his arms. As the sounds of the sirens got closer he could hear people all around him. All of the voices ran together and he could only pick out a few bits of conversation here and there.

Mostly they were asking what was going on, but he also heard the distinct sound of laughter. The sirens were now wailing in his ears and he heard a loud authoritive voice yelling for people to get back and he heard the woman screaming, "Get your fucking hands off me!"

He felt a hand on his shoulder and heard the voice ask him, "Man what the hell happened here?"

"She has mace!" he wailed at the voice.

"My partner already has her in the car man,' the voice said, "Come on buddy sit up, I need to flush your eyes."

Matt did as he was told. His hope for a miracle, cure all, end to the pain was not forthcoming though. After 15 minutes of having water run over his eyes and face he could finally see and breathe a bit easier.

The officer that had helped him had a bemused smile on his face as he held a towel out to him and the remains of Matt's cell phone. Matt snatched the items away from the officer and began drying himself as best he could. He couldn't tell if his cheeks were red from the mace or embarrassment at this point.

Matt noticed that a wrecker was loading up the Miata and that his Jeep had been moved into the gas station's parking lot. He looked at the cop and sighed.

"So what made her flip the fuck out?" he asked the officer, his vision was still blurry and he couldn't make out the cops name tag.

"Well," began the officer," it might have been your rudeness, the shock from the accident, or…"

The cop laughed a little bit before he continued, "Or it could have been the crank she was on, we found some in her car."

Matt's mind did a quick review of what he knew about the drug and he just shook his head. He reached into his back pocket, pulled out his insurance card, and held it up so the officer could see it.

"Please tell me that crazy bitch had one of these," he said as he handed it over.

"Oh yeah she has insurance on the vehicle," the officer said as he took the card," or at least her boyfriend has anyways."

Matt started to breathe a sigh of relief but the officer shook his head, "I wouldn't start feeling too comfortable right now buddy, her boyfriend just called and reported the car stolen."

"What the fuck?" Matt asked.

"Yeah it happens all the time," explained the cop," these druggies call each other anytime they see something happening, in this case druggie A called druggie B to let him know his car was getting towed."

Matt swore under his breath and started shaking his head back and forth. This day was going from bad to worse fast.

"So what happens now?" he asked.

"Well I take your information, his information, and then I file a report. Meanwhile another officer takes the boyfriend's stolen vehicle report and we pass everything over to the prosecuting attorney," the officer said, "What you have to do is report this to your insurance company and let them deal with it."

The officer continued, "She is under arrest for assault, driving under the influence, and stealing the car. The PA will want to talk to you in the next week or so about this whole thing."

Matt hung his head in resignation.

"Thanks, man," he told the officer.

"Oh we are not done yet buddy, I have a few questions for you and I need to get your side of the story here."

Matt told the officer his version of the events while the cop took several notes. When the officer told Matt he had to take his cell phone as evidence he only shrugged.

After a few minutes of relating his story and filling out a statement, Matt was back in his Jeep and pulling onto Highway 28 from Highway 50 to cover the last few miles to his parent's house.

He turned off onto his parents gravel road and was feeling thankful that soon he would be able to take a shower, get some aspirin, and get a well deserved nap. His feelings of gratitude even allowed him to overlook the smell of cow shit as he neared the house.

His father had decided to get involved in the cattle business last year and his dad, being his dad, had gone all out on the project. He purchased an automatic water dispenser and feeder. He had built a barn and installed cattle guards and gates along the road. The kicker to the whole thing was his father had only bought ten cows.

The last time Matt had been home he asked his dad why he only got a few cows and his father had told him that he wanted to raise them. Matt's innocent question resulted in the most disturbing conversation he had ever been a part of.

His father had explained to him, in depth, the process of artificial insemination. His dad was even nice enough to produce several magazines and catalogs where the semen could be purchased from, these included full color pictures of the donors, and customer testimonials.

Matt had never felt so detached from his family. His younger brother had bought three of the cows and was going into business with his father. Matt felt trapped as his brother and father argued over which semen to buy. All he could do to keep his sanity intact was to continue pounding down beer after beer. After fourteen of them he was actually participating in the conversation and arguing his point as to why his father should go with the bull's semen that he randomly picked out.

Matt had felt a moment of triumph when his father picked up the phone and ordered the stock he had suggested. Apparently all it took to decide on which bull juice to get was a good picture of the donor and a case of beer.

The Jeep bounced as he passed over cattle guard after cattle guard, and Matt could see a few of the beasts all gathered around a large tree in one of his dad's fields. He remembered his dad telling him that they were going to butcher their first cow in mid August. Matt was glad he would be back in Los Angeles by then, the thought of the killing and cleaning did not appeal to him at all.

When the house came into sight he was happy to notice that someone, most likely his dad and brother, had finally repaired the deck and stained it a nice cherry red color. Originally his father had insisted on a natural finish, which looked good until it started to mold and crack. For some unexplained reason his dad had used a stain without any type of water proofing and, if you asked him, he did it on purpose.

Matt pulled the Jeep onto the lawn next to the back door and turned off the engine. He could hear birds chirping up in the trees and the cattle grunting in the field as he pulled out a long unused key to unlock the door.

"Hello," he yelled after he got inside, "I'm here."

Silence was the only response to his greeting so he grabbed his bags and set them just inside the door before he began looking through the house. On the kitchen table he found a note written in his mother's spidery script.

Matt, sorry we're not here. Your brother needed Dad's help working on his truck. We will be home tomorrow. Love you, Mom.

Matt set the note back on the table and smiled. He had a day to rest and relax, without having to feign interest in his dad's hobbies, and he planned to be out the door very early the next morning even though it was a Sunday.

He went into the bathroom and swore in frustration when he couldn't find any aspirin. Matt was almost out of the door and heading back into town when a thought came to him. He went into his parent's bedroom and examined his mother's medication.

There he found a bottle of Vicodin and grabbed two of the magical pills. After washing them down with a glass of milk from the fridge he grabbed a towel and returned to the bathroom.

After a long hot shower he could feel the effects of the narcotic starting to take hold. He moved his luggage into his old room and changed into a pair of shorts and t-shirt.

As he was drifting off to sleep he briefly thought about Justin. He hoped he had cut back on his drinking like he said he would.

"And there will be signs in sun and moon and stars, and on the earth distress of nations in perplexity because of the roaring of the sea and the waves, people fainting with fear and with foreboding of what is coming on the world. For the powers of the heavens will be shaken. And then they will see the Son of Man coming in a cloud with power and great glory. Now when these things begin to take place, straighten up and raise your heads, because your redemption is drawing near."

- Luke 21:25-28

7

ONE LITTLE, TWO LITTLE, THREE LITTLE INDIANS

Outside of Rosebud, Missouri – June, Present Day

Sean pressed the rifle tight against his shoulder and slowly placed his finger on the trigger. He did his best to slow his breathing and calm his shaking nerves. The target, an overweight and younger kid in his class, moved through the woods completely unaware of what was about to happen.

He had picked his sniping position out the day before and had been laying down on top of the small ridge for the last hour, just waiting for one of the other kids to come by. He licked his dry lips, took a deep breath and then held it. In a few more seconds, he would have his first kill.

Sean felt a tingle run down his spine in anticipation. His target stopped moving and adjusted the backpack he was wearing, the flab from his belly causing a small momentary struggle with a strap. The armed boy couldn't stop the smile that spread across his face. The soon-to-be killer allowed another second to slip by, relishing the rush he was feeling.

A sudden snapping of twigs from behind him was the only warning Sean had before he heard a sharp *CRACK* from another weapon. Pain erupted from the back of his head and the world hurtled toward him from the force of the impact.

Sean's rifle fell from his hands without a shot being fired. He gingerly reached back and felt a bruise already forming. He looked at his hand and it was covered with green paint. *James got me,* he thought.

He rolled over onto his back and saw his friend leaning against a tree. James had a cocky look on his tan face and was pulling out a cigarette from a pack in his tactical vest. His dark spiked hair had some leaves and other vegetation clinging to it. Sean glared up at him while pulling out a handkerchief to wipe the paintball remains from his head.

"I almost had Lewis," Sean growled in pain.

James handed him a lit cigarette and pulled another one out of his pack. Sean took a few drags and shook his head to help clear it. *That paintball did a number on me,* he thought.

"You were nowhere close ta' hittin' me," he heard Lewis pant from somewhere off to his left, "I saw you clear as day."

"Bullshit," said James as Lewis made his way up to them, the cigarette dancing on his lips, "Your fat ass had no idea where he was until you saw me waving at you."

"Why couldn't you have waited a few more seconds?" Sean groaned to James as the more muscular boy helped him up.

"That isn't how we do it. If you want to join, you have to show us you can handle yourself when the zombies crawl out of the ground."

"I know, I know!" Sean complained as he started walking back towards camp.

He had heard about their group right after school started and decided that the idea of a group of people pretending to fight zombies sat well with him. It was called 'Zombification Orientation and Defense' or Z.O.D. for short. There were seven members in the middle school he attended and Lewis and him finally approached them in February about joining.

There were a few conditions the members had set, one of which Sean had yet to accomplish. That little condition was getting someone out during a paintball match. Sean was an excellent marksman, but it always seemed that he was spotted before he could get a shot off!

"Look on the bright side," James said as he blew smoke out of his nose, "we were the only three left. You outlived the rest of your team."

"Yeah, but I'm still not Z.O.D."

"You will be," Lewis said, "If I can do this, so can you!"

Sean handed the rest of the cigarette to Lewis, all he ever could manage was one or two drags and then he would feel lightheaded and a bit sick to his stomach. Lewis inhaled deeply and blew some smoke rings in James's face. The older boy gave him a disgusted look and punched him in the shoulder.

"Don't sweat it, man," James remarked as he put his cigarette out against a tree, "Fuck, it took me six months to get in and now I'm in charge of my age group."

"And what a great and glorious leader you are, James!" joked Lewis as he rubbed his shoulder. The chubby kid finished his cigarette and stomped it out.

The faint sound of a bell rang out from the direction of their campsite. The boys looked at each other and smiled. The bell meant lunch would be done soon and Emma made some of the best food they had ever tasted.

"Last one there is a shit eater!" yelled James.

As one they grabbed their paintball guns and launched themselves towards camp. Sean easily wound his way through the woods, staying ahead of his friends. Behind him he could hear crashing and cursing as they tried to match his pace.

"I might not be able to shoot someone, but I can outrun any of you!" Sean taunted behind him.

He continued to weave his way between trees and leap over smaller obstacles as he ran. He only slowed his pace when he saw the break in the trees that led to the campground. He could still hear James running behind him but heard no sign of Lewis. Undoubtedly his physique was to blame on his position in the race.

Just before Sean stepped into the clearing he heard a loud *CRACK* and then felt another paintball hit him in the back of the head. This time the shot made him fall facedown onto the forest's floor.

He was just starting to get up when James sprinted past him. The older boy turned around and gave him a salute along with that cocky smile of his.

"You might be able to outrun us, but it's hard to outrun a paintball!"

Sean felt anger rising up in him and, before he could stop, he launched himself at James. His friend had a look of surprise on his face as Sean tackled him to the ground and started throwing punches at him.

James moved his hands in a flurry, blocking most of the blows that Sean aimed at him. The few that did land were only glancing and was no doubt hurting Sean worse than him. James grabbed Sean's left arm and bucked as hard as he could after hooking his leg around his friend's ankle. The fraction of a second Sean was in the air was all he needed to roll away from him and, using his arm as leverage, put Sean's face in the dirt.

"Calm down, man… Shit! It was supposed to be fucking funny!" James sputtered, leaping to his feet.

"Fuck you!" yelled Sean as he pushed himself off the ground. He stood facing James with his fists clenched tightly in front of him.

James could see scrapes and cuts on his friends knuckles, some were bleeding freely. He was thankful none of the punches had hit him! He knew he was stronger than Sean, but the shear ferocity of the attack had almost overwhelmed him and it certainly caught him off guard.

"Seriously, calm the fuck down," said James.

Sean's head was pounding so hard he could barely hear what James was saying. He could feel rage rising and falling away inside of him like waves in the ocean. Sean closed his eyes so tight tears formed and fought to get his shaking limbs back under control.

James had seen Sean lose his temper several times over the last year. It was one of the things that had made Sean such an outsider at school. James, who was much more accepting than most, even had trouble at times hanging out with the volatile red head.

Lewis was actually the only real friend Sean had in school. Whether it was the case of a couple of outcasts just hanging out or not was anyone's guess, however the two always seemed to be having fun together.

Sean began to breathe easier and slowly lowered his hands down to his side. He wiped away some of the tears from his eyes before opening them and looking at James. The older boy had a scowl across his face and looked ready to strike back at him any moment.

"I'm sorry," he said, "I can't stop myself sometimes."

"Yeah, I know," James began," but if you ever take a swing at me again I'll kick your—"

The older boy was interrupted by Lewis, who came jogging out of the woods with his head down and panting, running into the back of him. James was pushed to the ground in front of Sean by the momentum and Lewis landed face first where James had been standing.

Sean was surprised for a moment but then broke into laughter. The sight of Lewis with his backpack laying on his head and moaning was just too much for him. James rolled over onto his back, all the while sputtering and cursing, and rubbed his right knee.

"Lewis, you fat fuck!" mumbled James as he stood up, "What in the hell is wrong with you?"

Lewis flailed around until he got the backpack off and then he sat up, still panting heavily and wheezing a bit. He took in a few deep breaths of air as Sean handed him his canteen. The chubby blonde kid gulped down a few drinks and looked sheepishly at James, "I didn't wanna' miss lunch."

James stared down at his fellow Z.O.D. teammate in astonishment. The look on their two faces caused Sean to start laughing again. Soon the other two joined in and James held his hand out toward Lewis.

"Well come on then," the older kid said with a grin as he helped him up, "Let's get you fed before you waste away."

Clyde Zelch, along with his wife Emma, had started the Pioneer Homestead & Village at Zelch Farms after he returned from a long overseas tour of the Middle East. His experience in the military and then law enforcement had paved the way for him to join the peace forces that operated, and trained the local forces, in that region of the world after Operation Desert Storm.

When he returned home he decided that he wanted to live a simpler life. His wife, who had always been very supportive of him, helped him out as much as she could while still taking care of their children.

Clyde built several small wooden cabins on their property with the help of his sons and slowly the Pioneer Homestead & Village was born. To generate income on the property, the couple treated it like a tourist spot. The General Store carried various wares, most of which were homemade items that Emma created such as jellies and lye soap. Small cabins could be rented by campers for a nominal fee, but one of the biggest attractions the family offered was classes. These classes consisted of many basic survival skills that had been mostly lost with the coming of modern conveniences, along with a Concealed Carry Class that was mandatory in Missouri for anyone who wanted to carry a hidden firearm on them.

This weekend was one of the biggest events he would hold all year. He had more than thirty campers for the weekend and most of them had signed up for one class or another. On top of those he also had organized a paintball match earlier in the day and planned on having a dance later in the evening after the chinking class finished the latest cabin. Now, however, he wanted to see how the current class would handle the visual demonstration.

"Then you just slowly pull down on the skin like so," Clyde said as he deftly removed the skin from the rabbit and placed it on the wooden stump next to him.

Some of the girls in the class gasped and the boys laughed at their response. Clyde managed to hide his grin as he sternly barked, "Settle down! Everyone needs to know the basics of skinning. You can ruin a lot of good meat if you don't know what you're doing."

The class, which consisted of a mixture of boy and girl scouts along with a club called Z.O.D., slowly quieted—although a few snickers could still be heard. Clyde waited a few more moments and then slipped his knife into the carcass, not surprising there were more gasps and muttering as blood spilled over the picnic table he was using for the demonstration.

Sean found it hard to concentrate as the class continued. It wasn't that he found the subject matter dull or boring, quite the contrary he was fascinated with it all, he just couldn't focus because of Elizabeth.

She was in the eighth grade, like James, and was here as part of her Girl Scouts troop yearly skill building weekend. Sean had developed an instant crush when he first saw her after he started school. Her brown eyes and soft smile made him crazy when he looked at her, and her black hair fell across her cheeks in a way that heightened that smile. He had been too shy to try to talk to her until the last day of school before summer break.

He had walked up to her in the hallway while she was with some of her friends before the last class of the day and said, "Hi." She had smiled at him and said, "Hello." Then his mind went blank! He had a conversation all planned out and hearing her voice completely erased it from his mind. He stood there awkwardly for a few seconds and then just turned around and walked to his locker.

Behind him he could hear her friends laughing at him and he felt his face flushing with embarrassment. Lewis had witnessed the whole thing and had come over to his locker to try to console him. Since then Sean had promised himself that the next time he saw her he would have the conversation he had originally planned. But now, here in the middle of the woods and around all of these other people, he found himself too afraid to say anything to her.

James nudged Sean with his elbow, snapping him out of his thoughts. He leaned over and whispered, "So are you going to have the balls to ask her to dance tonight?"

Sean glared at him, "It's not about balls! It's about finding the right time to talk to her."

Lewis, who had been standing behind the two, leaned in and said, "Are you sure it's not about balls? Because the whole 'finding the right time' line is used by people who don't have balls."

James giggled and Sean felt his face getting red. He threw Lewis a dangerous look and muttered, "You know who doesn't have balls? You, that's who! Maybe they got lost under your stomach, fat-ass!"

James stopped giggling and looked at Lewis. He had never heard Sean make such blatant fun of his friend before about his weight. If Lewis was hurt by the remark the smile on his face hid it well as he replied, "My balls are so big they're holding my gut up, bitch!"

The tension was broken when all of them laughed. There were several pairs of eyes that turned to the trio and then they heard Clyde say, "By all means keep goofing off. If you hit the bladder while you're doing this in a minute you'll wish ya' woulda' watched me doin' it first."

"We have to actually DO THIS?!" one of the girl scouts squeaked.

Clyde kept a neutral look on his face as he reached under the table and pulled out a hunting bag full of squirrels he had filled that morning. Even though his outward expression remained stern, he was smiling on the inside as he dumped out the dead rodents. He let the silence hang in the air for a moment before he finally grinned.

"Nah' you don't have to if ya' don't want to, but this'll be good experience for anyone who wants it," said Clyde. "Those that wanna' pass on it can go ahead on over to where Emma will be starting the next soap making class."

"Thank God!" said the same Girl Scout.

Clyde rolled his eyes and shook his head. He always found it difficult to accept that young people had no idea on how much they relied on technology. He looked around at all the people in the class and wondered how many of them would survive if there was some kind of catastrophe and technology became unreliable. His eyes picked a few likely candidates out and then settled on Sean, a kid he had worked with before and who had showed remarkable aptitude in tracking and shooting, and sighed. *One in ten it looks like,* he thought. *At least that gives humanity some hope.*

The glow from the lanterns lit the clearing in an eerie paleness. It was a paleness that reminded Sean of every horror film set in the woods he had ever seen. The music was loud enough to chase away any awkward silences that could fill the gap in conversation though and his confidence was slowly beginning to harden.

James was in a group of seven kids that were dancing and laughing amongst themselves. Lewis, much to everyone's surprise, was a dancing machine. He flowed with a fluid grace that dumbfounded onlookers.

Sean smiled when he saw his friend having such a good time. It was rare for Lewis to be so good at something that required such dexterity and control. Tonight, all eyes were on him it seemed.

When the song ended there was a scattering of applause and James slapped Lewis on the back a few times while smiling and saying something to him that Sean couldn't hear. Whatever it was made his friend smile and laugh.

Sean slowly worked his way towards Elizabeth, who was getting a glass of lemonade, all the while running through his head what he wanted to say. As he neared her she turned around and bumped into him, spilling the sugary beverage down the front of her shirt.

"I'm sorry," Sean yelped as he pulled a wet wipe from his pocket.

"Oh, God, it's sticky," she said while holding her hand out for the wipe.

Sean tore the package open and handed it to her. She rubbed her chest a few times and then tossed the wipe away in frustration. "Ugh!" Elizabeth groaned, "It's not working. I need to take a shower now and I didn't bring an extra shirt with me."

"I have one you can use!" Sean offered.

"Let me guess, it's something red or black?" she asked.

Sean's mind froze again. Was she asking because she liked the colors? Or did it mean she paid attention to what he wore and she knew he liked red and black? What shirt did he have for tomorrow?

"Uhhh—"

Sean was interrupted by a loud squeal from the speakers and the sound of feedback echoing through the woods. Everyone turned to the small stage where a microphone had been set up. Sean breathed a sigh of relief when Elizabeth turned her back to him.

Miss Hevener, the Girl Scouts Troop Leader, was fighting with the microphone while trying to turn the speaker away from her. After another high pitched whine and mutterings from the crowd she finally got it under control.

"I have a few announcements to make but first, I want to take some time to thank Clyde and Emma Zelch for having us all here this weekend. Let's show them our appreciation for their hospitality," Miss Hevener began clapping and all of the Girl Scouts joined in. Sean started to applaud after Elizabeth and he noticed that some of the Boy Scouts were whooping and hollering as well.

"Okay," began Miss Hevener, "Settle down now and let's get these over with so we can go back to having fun. First thing to announce is a reminder about the youth softball game. We are having it next Saturday at Memorial Park in Owensville at three."

Elizabeth cocked her head toward Sean and asked, "Are you going to be there?"

Sean thought he heard a trace of hopefulness in her voice and his heart leapt to his throat. He cleared his throat and mumbled, "Yeah, sure will."

"The following Sunday," Miss Hevener continued, "Our troop will be having a bake sale and car wash to cover the cost of—"

The ground suddenly shifted under Sean's feet and he began to topple over. He saw Elizabeth lose her footing at the same time and held out his hands to catch her as she swayed toward him. She let out a small yelp as she landed heavily in Sean's arms and the two fell in the dirt.

They stared at each other in confusion and then tightly held on to the other's body when they felt the ground continuing to shake. All around them, people were lying in the dirt. Some were quiet and had blank expressions on their faces while others looked horrified and screamed. Loud popping sounds began to echo all through the forest.

One of the boy scouts across the clearing had managed to stay on his feet and Sean watched as his body convulsed in an effort to maintain his balance during the earthquake. He made eye contact with him for the briefest of moments, just long enough to witness one of the trees break in half and land on the poor kid's shoulder. The weight of the timber jerked his body brutally to the side and there was no time for him to even cry out before his spine was broken and his torso nearly torn away from his pelvis.

A shower of blood and other bodily fluids landed on the people closest to the unfortunate soul and more screams erupted from those who had been paralyzed only moments before. Sections of the ground cracked everywhere around Sean and Elizabeth and the two struggled against the violent shaking as they tried gaining their footing.

The popping sounds grew into a roar and Sean could see trees all around them coming apart or just falling over. Looking over at the stage, he saw Miss Hevener pinned underneath one of the speakers and she began screaming for help. Sean could see blood forming in a small pool around her and started crawling toward the trapped woman.

"Don't leave me!" Elizabeth screeched while trying to grab his leg as Sean moved toward the wounded lady.

"Stay close to me!" Sean countered while he continued his rescue attempt.

Sean glanced back just to make sure that she was following him. Elizabeth had her head down and was just rocking back and forth and whimpering. Sean started to turn toward Miss Hevener again when he saw a large tree limb begin to crack above the frightened girl.

"Elizabeth, NOOO!" Sean used all of his fear to fuel his speed as he launched himself toward her. She looked at him numbly when she heard her name and never saw the branch as it began to fall.

Sean dove into her, knocking her backwards and coming to

rest on her lap. The limb landed on his legs, sending explosions of pain throughout his entire body. Elizabeth screamed and tried to roll the log off of him, the jostling causing more agony to erupt from his crushed legs.

"Help me!" Elizabeth yelled, her voice mingling with all of the similar calls for aid, and she sobbed uncontrollably when no one answered her pleas.

"I can't move it, Sean!" she wailed.

Sean felt himself losing consciousness and he did his best to keep from crying when he looked at her. "Are you okay?" he asked her.

She looked at him in disbelief at his question. He was pinned under a tree and he was asking her how she was doing? Before she could respond Lewis appeared out of nowhere.

"Push it off him!" he yelled as he put his weight against the branch. Sean felt more pain when Elizabeth started helping and was about to beg for them to stop when James jumped over his field of vision and added his strength to their task.

Sean could hear his friends grunting from the effort and the ground stopped shaking as suddenly as it started. After what seemed like minutes to the injured kid, the branch finally shifted enough and Sean was free.

His legs throbbed and each beat of his heart sent waves of burning agony to his feet. He drew in long slow breaths as he saw the destruction around him. Few trees were left standing and most everyone was holding some kind of wound.

The smell of blood mixed with the earthy aroma of the forest. Sounds of crying, screaming and other whimpering created an unsettling chorus around the children and they closed their eyes and huddled together.

He looked over to where Miss Hevener was laying. The pool of blood was now being soaked up by the ground and her matted hair. She stared unblinking at him and it took a few moments for Sean to realize that she was dead. He had trouble looking away from her until a flash of light quickly crossed his face.

When Sean turned his eyes away from the dead woman to follow the light he saw that the only building still standing was the simple wooden church. Firelight reflected off of the single pane of stained glass at the base of the cross on top of the structure.

Even though he was surrounded by death and smoke, the sight brought him a small amount of comfort.

The earthquake was a localized event, and even though the magnitude at the epicenter was estimated to be over an 8 on the Richter Scale it was not felt more than five miles away. This left a lot of geologists scratching their heads in confusion. The event was too large to be called a microquake and yet there was no explanation as to why it wasn't felt, or why it didn't even register, further away. This type of phenomenon had become more and more frequent during the last few months and left a lot of questions unanswered.

Even though the destruction and loss of life was always severe, people in the affected areas would always remark how strange it was that churches never seemed to be damaged by the quakes.

"Train yourself to be godly. For physical training is of some value, but godliness has value for all things, holding promise for both the present life and the life to come."

- 1 Timothy 4:7-8

ASHES! ASHES! WE ALL FALL DOWN

Owensville, Missouri – June, Present Day

The sunlight hurt his eyes and the roaring cheers from proud parents caused his head to throb so much he wished his eyes would just burst from their sockets. Justin looked at his watch for the sixth time in less than ten minutes and cursed under his breath.

When Matt had invited him out to watch a softball game it had seemed like a fun idea. That was before Justin woke up with a hangover that he couldn't seem to shake, no matter how many sips of vodka he took from the flask he had in his shirt pocket.

He had only meant to drink a little last night, he vaguely remembered. He couldn't recall what had pushed him past a mellow buzz into the stage of passed-out in his backyard though.

He shrugged the thought away and took another quick

drink from his fast emptying flask, all the while ignoring the looks he was getting from those sitting around him. When his drinking problem first started he tried hiding it, but after a few months it was just easier to ignore people than to come up with more creative ways of concealing his alcoholism.

Justin lit a cigarette and took a long drag, blowing out the smoke as carefully as he could to try to avoid getting it close to the kids. He leaned back in the stands and rested his arms on the seat above him, glancing at his watch again and then looking toward the parking lot next to the baseball field.

He recognized almost everyone, it was a small town after all, and there were still a lot of folks that talked to him as if nothing ever happened. As if it was all forgivable, his actions and... Hers.

Justin pulled his gatsby over his face and closed his eyes while leaning his head back. He wished that Matt would hurry up and get to the park. After the game he was sure his friend would take him to a late lunch and then maybe they would hit a bar.

The sharp crack of a bat hitting a softball was quickly overshadowed by another eruption of cheers. Justin closed his eyes a little tighter while taking another long pull from his cigarette.

This time when he exhaled he didn't care who was offended by the smoke. He opened his eyes a slit when the cheering subsided and sat up while groaning against the pain in his head.

He pulled the flask out again and shook it, he couldn't hide the look of disappointment and worry on his face when he realized he only had a few drinks left in the container. He slowly unscrewed the top and hoped Matt had a cooler full of beer with him.

Matt got a later start than he had wanted. After his morning shower he called his wife and the conversation went from pleasant to heated when he told her that he would be out in Missouri for at least another week.

He was delayed even further when he ran into his parents

coming up the driveway as he was leaving. They insisted on talking to him at length about their morning excursion into town and his dad asked for his help with the cows.

He was finally able to break away from them a little after noon and hit one of the local grocery stores in Owensville. He made it a point to fill up his cooler with only water and sodas instead of beer. It was close to 1 p.m. when he pulled into the parking lot next to the baseball field.

Matt sat in the rented Jeep for a few moments while he scanned the crowd looking for Justin. He finally spotted him sitting in the second row of seats from the bottom and drinking out of a flask.

Matt clenched the steering wheel in anger and shook his head in frustration. Justin had told him that he would be sober today so they could talk about the upcoming trial and some other issues about the future.

He climbed out of the vehicle and slammed the door hard enough to make the Jeep sway. He grabbed the small cooler and started walking toward the seats when a familiar face caught his attention out of the corner of his eye.

A man wearing dirty overhauls was carrying two large coolers, one on top of the other, toward the bleachers. Despite his anger towards Justin, Matt couldn't stop the flood of happiness that welled up in him and he smiled.

"Well hello, Michael!" Matt yelled as he hurried up behind him.

The large man turned around so fast that melted ice water sloshed from out of the top cooler. He smiled when he saw Matt coming toward him and set his load on the asphalt.

"Matt!" he said, running up to his old friend with his arms outstretched, "Good ta' see ya'!"

Matt managed to set his cooler down before he was picked off of his feet. He felt his breath leave his body as the larger man hugged him. Even though it hurt like hell, Matt smiled and did his best to return the embrace. Matt would never forget how much the man holding him had sacrificed.

Michael had been one of the best high school linebackers in the country. There was a long line of colleges that wanted him and his future looked like it would go anywhere he wanted it to take him. That future turned into only a dream the night Matt's mother had gotten a flat tire.

Michael, who had always been a nice guy, had seen her on the side of the road and pulled over to help her change the tire. After he was done, Matt's mom tried giving him ten dollars and he refused. While she was insisting on giving him money, some things fell out of her purse and her compact makeup rolled into the roadway.

On instinct she had went after it and Michael barely managed to push her out of the way of an oncoming car. Even though he had been fast to react, she still suffered a broken leg from the impact. That was only a scratch compared to what happened to Michael.

He was flown to a hospital in St. Louis, was resuscitated twice while in flight and died a third time while in the emergency room. The third time is what changed him. The doctors said that his brain was without oxygen for seven minutes and any chance of recovery was gone.

Although Michael beat the odds, he suffered from severe brain damage and had to learn to do even the most basic of tasks again. That he could even speak was considered a miracle by his parents and they renewed their faith in the church, becoming die hard Catholics.

After they both were killed in a car accident a few years later, the former priest of the Catholic Church in Owensville took the young man under his wing and gave him a job as the church's grounds keeper.

Matt would forever be grateful and, unknown to his parents or wife, he would send money each month to the church to help cover the cost of anything Michael might want or need. He would also send the gentle man a Christmas and birthday card each year and would call him once in a while.

"That's enough, man!" Matt gasped while patting Michael on the shoulder to put him down.

The large man was still smiling when he set him back on his feet. Matt took a deep breath and looked into Michael's deep blue eyes. He felt a hint of sadness for what he had been through since the accident and felt a lump forming in his throat.

"Ya' here ta' see Justin and watch da' game, Matt?"

"Yeah, that's what I'm doing. I got in last week and stopped by the church to visit you, but no one was there."

"Dat' musta' been Wednesday. Da' Fadder' and me shop on dat' day."

"Well at least I get to see you now! Where are you taking those things?" Matt said while gesturing to the coolers.

"I'm takin' um' ta' da' Fadder'. He's helpin' out wit' da' game since Miss Hevener died."

Matt winced when he was reminded of the tragedy of the past week. A lot of minor injuries and two deaths had occurred at Pioneer Village. He didn't know the Boy Scout who lost his life, but he was very familiar with Jessica Hevener. The two had dated briefly in high school and it had not ended on a happy note.

"Well, let me walk with you and you can introduce me to Father Murray. I want to meet the man who looks after you when I'm not around," Matt said while picking up his small cooler.

"Dat' be okay. You'll like da' Fadder', he seems real nice ta' da' ladies and kids."

"He sounds like a good man." Matt remarked as he started following Michael through the crowd of people at the park.

Michael slowly turned around and looked at him with those piercing blue eyes of his and, for a moment, Matt thought he saw a flicker of hate burn in them. He stared back at Michael and felt a chill run down his spine when he spoke.

"He's nice but he ain't no good man. He's agunna' be chased by da' demons jus' like everyone else."

Sean sat down stiffly on the lowest level of the bleachers, his sore legs barely managing the walk from the car. When he had reached the hospital after the earthquake last week it had surprised everyone to learn his legs had not been broken, only badly bruised and sprained.

The whole trip to the emergency room was a blur to him and he could only remember bits and pieces after the tree had been rolled off of him. He knew that Clyde and been the one that carried him down to the waiting ambulance, but little else.

Sean looked around and started waving when he spotted Lewis carrying a sport bag into the dugout on the right side of the field. He would normally have just ran up to his friend, but the short walk took more out of him than he wanted to admit and he realized that running would be out of the question for a long time yet to come.

When Lewis saw him he hastily set the bag down and jogged over. Even though it was only a short run, his pudgy friend was slightly gasping when he made it to the bleachers.

"Hey, Speedy! Glad ya' made it out today!" Lewis said while smiling.

"I wasn't going to miss this. I love every chance I have to see your fatass run!" He quipped back playfully.

"You're goin' to see a lot of that today, bitch! I just wish you could still play so I could stomp your ass!"

"We're on the same team, moron," Sean said while unscrewing his water bottle.

"Yeah, but I bet I'd get more runs than you," his friend said as he waved to a few more people in the crowd.

Before Sean could reply, the man above them blew out cigarette smoke and the boys got a lung full. Sean coughed a few times and then sneezed as his body tried to force the acrid smell out of his nostrils. Lewis seemed to not be bothered by it at all.

Sean started to turn around to yell at the offender. Lewis, seeing the dark look on his friend's face, hastily leaned down and whispered to him, "It's Justin Grady."

Sean closed his eyes and counted to ten in his head. He felt Lewis sit down next to him and heard him continue in a low voice, "That dude lost his shit after he found his wife doing someone else in their bed."

Sean remembered hearing the story when it came out in the news. He was surprised that such a nice man could be involved with anything so horrible. Sean had met Pastor Grady shortly after moving to Owensville at a charity event Father Murray dragged him to.

While Father Murray wandered around the tables and

booths, Justin Grady engaged him in conversation and both were surprised they had so much in common. Both loved fantasy novels and role-playing games, Irish music, and the woods.

Pastor Grady had even taken him fishing a few times and was the one who introduced him to Clyde and Emma Zelch. Sean actually considered Justin a friend, until all that bad shit happened and he stopped all contact with everyone.

Sean looked up at the former pastor and their eyes locked for a moment. The events of the past year had certainly left their mark on the once happy-go-lucky young man. His eyes looked dull and expressionless, while the smile that crossed his face looked more sad than happy when he registered who he was looking at.

Justin's speech was a little slurred and when he spoke it was barely above a whisper, "I heard what you did last week, Sean. Clyde told me how brave you were and how ya' saved that girls life."

Sean felt Lewis relax next to him in his seat when he responded, "Yeah, I don't know about brave. It was just something that I had to do. I didn't really think about it, I just knew I didn't want her to get hurt."

"It was badass! You should have seen him, it was like something out of a movie," Lewis proclaimed proudly while slapping his friend on the back.

"Is that right?" Justin mumbled while continuing to stare at Sean, "Well, it looks like we have the next action movie star growing up right here in Owensville. Ha!"

Justin laughed at his own joke while he unscrewed the top of his flask and then drained the rest of the booze into his mouth. When he looked down, the two boys were staring up at him. He couldn't tell if it was fear on their faces or disgust.

Justin coughed a few times to clear his throat and did his best to smile. He was about to apologize when more cheering started from the crowd. He looked up in time to see a teenage girl sliding into home base.

"That's the end of that game, Sean. I'm gonna' find Father Murray and get signed in," Lewis said to his friend and then to Justin, "It was good seeing you again Mister Grady. Take care!"

"Kick some ass, Lewis!" Sean called after his friend when he bounded away. He watched as Lewis picked up his sports bag and sprinted awkwardly to the dugout where his team was assigned.

Sean was grateful that Lewis had come out, he hadn't seen him in a few days and was missing the company. As he looked in the dugout he saw James running up from the parking lot, headed toward Lewis. Sean chuckled under his breath, his friend always seemed to run late for one reason or another.

Sean's thoughts were interrupted by Justin's voice, "It's good to see you're okay, Sean. It really is. Hell, it's just good to see you."

The boy looked back at the man and a genuine smile was on his face. Sean returned it and the former pastor slid down into the seat that Lewis had left vacant. Together they both sat there in silence and looked out across the field, watching the new teams take their place.

Sean thought about all the bad things that had happened to Justin and then he allowed himself a rare moment to reflect back on his own circumstances. He let a few memories of his mom and dad wash over him and he had a thought.

"Justin," he asked, "Does everything good turn to shit?"

The young man continued to watch the baseball field for a few moments before finally turning toward Sean. He looked intently at the boy and then at the ground while he dug a cigarette out of his pocket and replied, "Not everything good. Just everything that can hurt us, kid. Just everything that can hurt us."

"I'm glad you could make it, James!" Father Murray said as the teenager came running into the dugout, "We are ready to go here guys. Does anyone have any questions?"

"I do!" said Lewis raising his hand.

Thomas inwardly groaned, "Yes, Lewis?"

"Are we going to say a prayer?" asked the chubby kid.

Father Murray silently cursed himself. He had almost sent

them out on the field without even bothering to make an attempt at anything pious. Judy had his head all turned around.

"Of course we are, Lewis. Let's all bow our heads," Thomas closed his eyes and lowered his head, "Dear Lord, we come before you today as your humble servants. We ask that you hold each of us in your arms and keep us safe as we enjoy this game. We thank you for the beautiful weather and for the support of all of our friends and families through this past week. Guide us, O' Lord, and grant us thy mercy. Amen."

A chorus of amens echoed around him and he ushered the team out on the field. Even though a smile was on his face as he was going through the motions, his mind was in turmoil over the letter he had received yesterday.

Judy Fritte, the lady who had dropped off Sean a little over two years ago, had sent him a letter to appear for a paternity test. Well, the letter came from his attorney, but Judy had set the whole damn thing in motion.

He cursed himself again for being such a fool. How could he know that she would get pregnant and come after him for child support? They only had a one night stand and if she slept with a priest wouldn't it stand to reason she was a slut and sleeping with a lot of other men?

He still believed that there was only a very small chance that the kid could be his, but there was still that chance. At least the whole thing was being kept from his superiors… For now.

Father Murray shook his head in frustration and let a scowl creep across his face. He was at the end of his rope and this coming Wednesday he would get his blood taken. The thought that his livelihood might be taken from him sent a wave of anger coursing through his body. He kicked one of the benches so hard it toppled over, spilling equipment all around the dugout.

"That call did suck," said an unfamiliar voice.

Thomas turned toward the sound and did his best to hide the scowl. He saw Michael setting the coolers down outside the dugout with a stranger in tow. The man was handsome and his athletic frame carried more muscle than the priest's.

The man was smiling and held his hand out, "I'm Matt Anderson. We talked on the phone a few times about Michael."

Father Murray started shaking the offered hand and smiled back, "Mister Anderson! It is a pleasure to finally meet you. What brings you out to our little ball game today?"

"I'm in town to visit family and to testify at Justin Grady's trial next week. I thought while I was down I'd hang out with Michael, too." Matt said while releasing the handshake.

"He's da' one I been tellin' ya' bout', Fadder," Michael said as he came into the dugout carrying three root beers. He handed out the beverages and picked up the overturned bench.

"Thank you, bud!" Matt said cheerily as he opened his drink.

Father Murray set his on the bench, unopened. This was a blessing in disguise! While he went to St. Louis to get his court ordered blood work completed he could leave Michael in this man's hands for a few days.

"You were right, Michael. He is a very nice man and he came all the way out here to visit you and his friends. Why don't you take them shopping on Wednesday with you and after that out to dinner. My treat of course!" Thomas looked at Matt when he finished speaking.

"That sounds like fun, Michael. What do you think?" asked Matt.

The big man was smiling from ear to ear when he replied, "Dat' would be great, Matt! You and me and Justin and Sean and James and Elizabeth…"

"Whoa there, bud!" interrupted Matt, "I was just thinking me, you and Justin. I don't know these other people."

"Are you talking about the kids, Michael?" asked Father Murray.

"Well yeah Fadder'! Dey' won't be able ta' make it wit' us not dere' wit 'em," said the gentle man, sounding confused, "Don't ya' want em' ta' be safe?"

"Well of course I want them to be safe, Michael. I just don't think all of them need to go with you and your friend," the priest said.

Matt saw a lot of disappointment on his friends face. *He must really like those kids*, he thought. It was obvious to him that Father Murray was not going to budge on his stance of just the three of them going, but Michael didn't need to know that.

"Hey, why don't we see what they are doing? If they aren't

busy next week we can ask them to go with us. Of course I don't know how much fun they would have with us on the golf course…" Matt let his voice trail off when the disappointment on Michael's face changed to one of excitement.

"Golf? We gonna' play golf?" he exclaimed.

"I thought we could. The golf course is still close enough to town that you shouldn't have to worry about the kids being safe, right?" asked Matt.

"Yeah, it's close!" Michael smiled.

"Well there we go, I will see you in a few days and we can plan it all out. Is that okay?" Matt said to his friend.

"Dat' sounds good, Matt!" the larger man hugged him again, much gentler this time.

"Mister Anderson, it sounds like you have a lot of fun planned. I still insist on paying for dinner for the three of you. It's the least I can do for all of your generosity over the years," Thomas held his hand out to Matt again as he was speaking.

Matt shook it briefly, "Sounds great. I will stop in Monday morning and we can finalize everything. Now, if you'll excuse me, I'm going to go smack my friend Justin around."

"Certainly, please tell Grady that I'm here if he needs anything," the priest said as he turned his attention back to the softball game.

"Buh-bye, Matt! See you soon!" Michael said as he began to clean up the sports equipment in the dugout.

"See you soon, too!" Matt grabbed his small cooler and hurried away.

Matt had felt uneasy through the entire conversation with the priest, but he couldn't put his finger on any particular reason. It was just some kind of bad vibe that he was giving off.

He made his way toward the bleachers and noticed that Justin had moved down a seat and was talking to a kid who had what appeared to be some kind of bandages over his legs. His friend had a lit cigarette in his hand and both of them had very somber expressions on their faces.

Matt tried to bring back his anger at Justin for drinking, but his visit with Michael left him too happy for any other emotion to take control. When he saw how glassy-eyed Justin was he made a mental note to thank Michael later for putting him in such a good mood, otherwise he might have choked him.

When Justin saw him approaching he smiled and tried to stand up on unsteady feet. The kid grabbed him before he leaned too far forward. If it wasn't for that quick action, his friend would have toppled over.

"Sit your drunk ass down, man!" Matt half-joked as he came up to Justin.

"Oh I'm more than half!" his friend laughed uneasily as he sat back down.

"This is Sean. Good kid, I told you about him before," Justin said while patting the wounded hero on the shoulder, "Sean, this is Matt. My best friend."

"Hey," said the boy as he nodded in his direction.

The kid looked like he was deep in thought, or was concentrating really hard on the game that was being played. Matt plopped down next to Justin and opened his cooler. He kept a sidelong glance on his friend as he did so and didn't miss the look of disappointment when Justin saw all he had was water and soda.

Matt handed him a water bottle with a dramatic flourish and smiled when Justin slowly took it from him and rolled his eyes. Matt chuckled as he pulled out a 7-Up and tapped Sean on the shoulder a few times with it.

Sean turned toward him and eagerly took the beverage, "Thank you, sir."

Both Matt and Justin laughed. Justin said, "Drop the 'sir', Sean. He was in the Marine Corps and he worked for a living!"

The two men laughed more and Sean joined in. He didn't know what was funny, but he didn't want to offend either of them. He was at ease around the two and it felt to him like he knew Matt from somewhere, but he couldn't place it.

The three of them watched as the game continued.

The conversation between the two men turned to things that held no interest for the boy and he watched the game more intently. He couldn't hide his smile when Elizabeth waved at him when she came up to bat.

He waved back at her while bouncing in his seat and did his best to ignore Lewis and James making kissy faces at him. He was glad to see that the two of them seemed to be getting along so well.

After ten minutes of watching the game he got to see Lewis hit a ball over the head of the right fielder. His friend was almost at first base when the outfielder threw the ball over the head of the first basemen.

To Sean, and everyone else's surprise, Lewis rounded first and took off running toward second. When the basemen managed to get the ball he overthrew it and Lewis cleared second and was on third when the same outfielder threw the ball over the third basemen's head!

Everyone was screaming and cheering as Lewis ran to home plate. There was a lot of laughing in the stands, too, at the antics that had led up to the first run of the game. Sean was so happy for his friend he even stood up and applauded, despite the searing protest from his legs.

With his wide smile sparkling in the sunlight and his teammates around him slapping him on the back at the plate, Lewis looked at him and gave him a salute. Sean started to walk toward him and then... He *felt* it.

It felt like music was playing inside his body and that a chorus was rising up from his stomach. Every muscle tensed and relaxed over and over again, like it was dancing to the unheard melody he was feeling. His head rolled back on his shoulders as his eyes turned towards the sky. A light exploded in front of his face, blinding him. His body felt weightless to him and there was no pain in his legs anymore. He felt like he was floating off of the ground and then everything went black.

As suddenly as it started, it stopped. He felt like he was slammed back into his body as his weight returned. He crumbled to the ground and he felt a throbbing pain in his head and heard a high pitched squeal in his ears.

He had tears running down his face and he didn't know

why he was crying. As the squealing noise left his ears it was replaced by screams and yells from everywhere. When he managed to open his eyes he saw members of the crowd rushing toward the field where the bodies of several kids were laying still.

He noticed a few adults and all the younger kids slumped over in the bleachers, then he felt strong hands dragging him to his feet. His eyes focused on Matt, who was staring at him with wide eyes and a shaking lower lip, but he also saw Justin stumbling toward him.

The screams from all around blocked out any words the pair were trying to say to him. All over the park he saw people, mostly kids but a few adults, lying on the ground. Sean's gaze fell on Lewis. His friend was on his back among a cluster of other kid's bodies, with his right foot still on home plate.

Sean's breath turned shallow and he was shaking until he saw James and Elizabeth coming out of their dugout. He relaxed for just a moment and a sigh of gratitude escaped him. Some of his worry dissipated when it appeared that they were okay, although their open mouths and darting eyes betrayed the shock they were feeling.

Sean was halfway to them before he realized he had broken free of Matt's grasp and was running, without any pain in his legs. He slowed his pace suddenly to a fast walk, then to a few slow steps as he gingerly tested his weight on each of his feet.

He pulled the now loosened brace off of his right leg and stared at his skin. There was no indication that anything had ever been wrong with the limb. No discoloration or swelling was evident. Sean slowly looked around, his brain trying to process the scene.

A woman wearing grey sweatpants and a black sports top was kneeling on the ground and holding a young girl, maybe six or seven years old, close to her chest and was screaming for an ambulance in between guttural sobs.

Among all of the screams, all of the chaos that was unfolding around him, he could not look away from the child the woman was holding. He felt, more than saw, Elizabeth next to him. He knew that she was holding his hand with both of hers and was trying to pull him away from the field, yet all he could do was continue to stare at the small child.

Even though her eyes were wide open and vacantly staring, there was a smile on her dirt and tear streaked face. It was the most serene expression he had ever seen and a chill ran through him when his father's death grin came unbidden to his mind.

He didn't know what had just happened but he was sure that she, indeed everyone who was unresponsive, had felt the music. Sean feared that it had taken all of them a lot further than it did him.

Michael leaned against the dugout fence a few feet away from Father Murray and jumped up and down while Lewis was sprinting for home plate. The smile on the kid's face brought another wild round of clapping from the large man, his big hands sounding like steaks being pounded on a cutting board.

He looked over to make sure Father Murray had seen the miraculous event and then his face dropped in sadness when he saw the priest had his back turned to him and was whispering softly into a cell phone.

Michael didn't let his disappointment last long. He bolted out of the dugout with a can of root beer in his hand and headed to the kid to give him a hug and a drink. He was sure that Lewis would be thirsty after all of the running and wanted to have something for the kid. He only made it a few paces when he heard... *Him.*

Michael toppled over face first onto the field as the sweet voice spoke in his head. The large man rolled over on his back while listening to the voice as it assured him that everything was going to be okay.

Michael began sobbing when the voice answered his unspoken thoughts about the children. He knew it wasn't his place to question, but before he could stop himself he asked, "Why?"

The gentle and loving voice continued to speak to him, even as his arms and legs convulsed. Michael's thoughts became more coherent than they had been since the accident and, when he realized what was happening, he tried to yell out a warning to anyone that could hear him.

Before his thoughts could be vocalized everything exploded in light and he felt himself flying. He looked down at his body and felt all the worries of his old life slowly slip away as he soared through the sky.

"Michael! Come home!" He heard his mother and father yelling.

His soul flew toward the sound of their love.

His legs pumped faster than he ever imagined possible and he gasped for air as he sped around the bases. Lewis could feel his heart hammering in his chest and bursts of energy flowing to his legs.

He felt shaky when he came around third base and his vision narrowed when his eyes looked at home plate. All the sounds of cheering and yelling seemed to suddenly come from far away as everything but the plate became fuzzy in his mind.

His muscles felt like they were working against water as he neared the base, each step causing him to think that at any second he would see the catcher reach for a thrown ball to tag him out.

When he jumped on home plate all of his senses returned. He stood, stunned that he had actually made it on one hit, as most of his teammates rushed out of the dugout to greet him.

As they were slapping him on the back he noticed that even Sean had stood up on his wrecked legs to show how proud he was of him. Lewis smiled wider than he ever had before and gave his best friend a salute.

As he was lowering his hand he felt something warm and unseen wrap around him. He smelled fresh baked cookies and bread like his grandmother use to make when she was alive.

He closed his eyes as the warmth spread into him, flowed into him, and then carried him upwards toward a beautiful light. As he entered eternity he thought of his friends briefly, but the thought disappeared as suddenly as it came when he smelled his grandmother's hot cocoa and heard his grandfather singing "Amazing Grace."

Sister Anna Clair leaned back in one of the pair of oversized leather chairs in her office. She let out a low and silent yawn while covering her mouth with the latest edition of the *Albuquerque Journal*.

She set the paper on the oak stand next to her chair and removed her glasses to rub her tired eyes. She stifled another yawn with the back of her left hand and reached for her mug of tea with the other.

She had just placed the hot beverage to her lips when it happened. She felt tingles erupting all along her body, causing her skin to feel as if electricity was coursing through her veins, and a bright light exploded in front of her.

She heard voices of loved ones, lost long ago, calling out to her and tears flooded her face when she realized she was going home. She dropped the hot mug of tea on her lap, but by the time the liquid spilled onto her she was beyond feeling any pain.

Judy Fritte hummed a tune she had heard earlier that morning on the radio. She was relaxing in a chair next to her daughter's bed reading. Occasionally, she would reach out and adjust the blanket she had placed on her child when she had put her down for her nap.

The small blonde girl's chest rose and fell with each breath and Judy smiled every time Melissa made little noises in her sleep. The woman thought of all the things in her life that had changed since she had gotten pregnant.

She had wanted to be married before she had any children, but her indiscretion from a few years ago had changed all of that. Judy still had trouble believing that she had gotten knocked up by a priest.

Jake Dabner had been relentless when she started showing and despite her best efforts at trying to get him fired, he still remained employed at the children's home. Judy had since forgiven the man silently and didn't let his jibes get to her anymore. Even though she had lost her way for a while, she was now confident in her faith in God and in His love for her and her child.

Judy lifted her arms above her head and made soft moaning sounds as she stretched. She reached down to rub Melissa's back and just as she touched her child a bright light erupted in front of her eyes.

The scream stopped in her throat before she could let it loose, and the light created a glow of warmth that spread from her stomach to all of her extremities. She heard her daughter laughing and then was stunned when she heard a long silent voice utter, "Melissa! I'm your grandpa. Grab Mommy's hand and we can all go home."

Judy felt her daughter's tiny hand wrap around her finger, through the light she could make out the familiar face of her dad smiling at her. Spread out all around behind him was all of the people she had ever loved. They were all dressed in robes of the brightest white and were softly singing a song of eternal love and peace. Judy reached out toward her father and when they touched she knew she never had to worry about anything ever again.

"And he shall send his angels with a great sound of a trumpet, and they shall gather together his elect from the four winds, from one end of heaven to the other. Now learn a parable of the fig tree; When his branch is yet tender, and putteth forth leaves, ye know that summer is nigh: So likewise ye, when ye shall see all these things, know that it is near, even at the doors. Verily I say unto you, This generation shall not pass, till all these things be fulfilled. Heaven and earth shall pass away, but my words shall not pass away. But of that day and hour knoweth no man, no, not the angels of heaven, but my Father only."

- Matthew 24:31-36

IT'S RAINING, IT'S POURING, THE OLD MAN IS SNORING

Owensville, Missouri – June, Present Day

Matt and Father Murray were drenched in sweat. Their breath came in short, ragged gasps as they carried some adults and child after child into the church and gently laid the bodies in rows all along the inside walls.

Justin had did his best to help out the others who volunteered, but his inactivity over the last year left him out of shape and near to collapse after only a few hours of strenuous work. Matt, who knew his friend would have a heart attack before he stopped, finally had to tell him to go around town and round up any supplies he could.

After the occurrence at the park, it fast became obvious that local emergency crews were not equipped to deal with something of this magnitude. To make matters worse, the phenomenon had become worldwide and not just local. When it became apparent that hospitals and other medical facilities were overrun, the children and those adults affected were taken to local churches and schools where any local medical professionals volunteered their services.

Worried parents refused to leave their children's sides and the cramped conditions, coupled with the fear of what was going on, had caused tempers to flare and fights were becoming common.

The sky overhead was becoming filled with storm clouds and military aircraft. Highway 28 and Highway 50 were becoming a common sight for convoys of Army troops. News out of Fort Leonard Wood was that the National Guard had been called up to deal with a meltdown that was occurring at the Callaway Nuclear Power Plant, which was only about 65 miles north of Owensville.

As Justin drove through town in Matt's rented Jeep he took in the eerie quiet that was occasionally disrupted by distant rumbles of thunder. He had tried to call his friend Clyde numerous times and, when he could get a signal, it kept ringing until it went to voicemail.

He had turned off the radio a few minutes ago, the reports were becoming very disturbing and he had enough to handle without becoming overcome by the rising tide of paranoia that was grabbing ahold of people.

Justin was amazed at the lack of traffic on the streets. His first stop was a small store that specialized in ammo and liquor in the middle of town on Highway 28. He was disappointed at the amount of empty shelves that greeted him as he entered the establishment. The man, more of a kid really, behind the counter gazed at him briefly before turning his attention back to the small television that was on the counter.

"…puzzled by the illness. Doctor Yadav, from the Mayo Clinic, has said that there is no medical explanation thus far for the comatose state. In a written statement he further goes on to say 'The organs are in perfect condition and the brain has activity such as is common with those in REM sleep. Blood tests are still being done, but at this time nothing is out of the ordinary…" the news lady droned a report.

The former pastor noticed that all of the cheap booze was gone, as well as most of the ammunition. He grabbed two bottles of Drambuie and a bottle of Grey Goose vodka. He carefully set them on the counter and silently thanked Matt for giving him his debit card to use.

"Looks like you've been busy today," he joked with the cashier, "I don't suppose you have any .308 shells stashed back there somewhere do you?"

It took the kid a few moments to realize that he had been spoken to. Once he made eye contact with Justin he blinked several times, as if he was waking up from a dream. With shaking hands he ran the bottles under the bar code reader, swiping the Grey Goose multiple times before he was rewarded with a *beep* from the machine.

"Ummm… About the .308 shells?" Justin stammered.

"Nothing… I got nothing left, man," the clerk responded with a catch in his throat.

"Do you know where—" Justin started to ask but trailed off when the clerk turned back to the television again. He started to feel anger rise up in him until he saw tears sliding down the side of the kids cheeks.

As Justin was leaving the liquor store he heard the woman's voice on the TV, "Do you think there is any connection with the strange weather and earthquake phenomenon?"

He sat down in the driver's seat of the Jeep and opened the bottle of Grey Goose. He raised it to his lips and tilted the bottle up. As he swallowed he noticed a skinny man in swimming trunks with a towel over his bare shoulders give him a thumbs up. The world seemed like it was going crazy, so why be sober? He started the vehicle and drove toward the next store.

He turned into the parking lot of a hardware store and was not comforted by the scene. People were loading anything of value into their vehicles. He opened the door and stepped out, balancing on the running board of the Jeep, trying to wrap his vodka-numbed mind around what was happening.

Several people were loading big rolls of plastic wrap into their cars, while other's shouted and waved handfuls of cash in front of their faces. A few of the more desperate individuals tried to wrestle the plastic away from those who were trying to get it in their vehicles.

Justin was horrified as he watched an elderly grey-haired

man in blue jean overhauls get roughly pulled backwards from a beat-up looking green Ford truck by an overweight bald man, his ragged cut-off shorts peeking out from under the bottom of a dirty white t-shirt. The fat man snatched the roll of plastic from the old man's hands as a very thin and gaunt looking lady bent down to wrestle something else away from the poor guy's pocket.

"Hey! You! Stop it! Leave him alone!" Justin grabbed the tire iron from the back of the Jeep and rushed to where the attack was taking place. The bald man kicked the helpless man in the ribs as the woman pulled something, which looked like duct tape, from his hands.

"Drop it!" Justin screamed as he got close. The fat man looked up with dull and vacant eyes, spittle frothing from his lips, and roared something unintelligible at him. The woman saw the tire iron and raised her hand, pointing at the weapon Justin held in the air.

"He gotta' wheel-changer, Clay!" She yelped.

Justin could see the woman was missing several teeth, and those she had left appeared to be dark and rotting. *Just my luck,* Justin thought, *I'm dealing with a couple of fucking tweakers.*

"I got this, Carol!" Clay snapped at the woman and then to Justin, "Get the fuck outta' here before ya get yer' ass stomped, cocksucker!"

Justin couldn't think straight. Whether it was from the booze, fear, or just his hatred at what he saw the couple do to the old man, he didn't know. Without worrying about the consequences, he swung the tire tool as hard as he could at Clay's leg.

A sickening *thomp* noise sounded as the makeshift weapon connected with the man's leg. He let go of the plastic roll and grabbed the injured appendage, all the while screaming out in pain. The woman let out a howl, a noise that sounded so primal that Justin almost dropped the steel weapon in his hand to cover his ears.

She lunged at him and he lashed out with the tire changer. The blow caught her on her left side, just where her bottom two ribs were. She crumbled without making a sound and held her side, her eyes blinked at him in rapid succession and then she started moaning. Justin dropped the tire tool in disgust at himself when he saw some of her ribs were breaking the surface of her skin.

The former pastor hastily helped the older man stand up, trying his best to ignore the wails of pain from the pair of meth heads he injured. Justin opened the door to the Ford and eased him onto the driver's seat, where he sat gasping for breath. The younger man retrieved the plastic roll and tape, he saw the older man staring at him and fidgeting with his glove box while he picked up the almost stolen items.

"I'm so sorry that—" Justin began when the old man stuck a black, newer looking, pistol in his face.

"Throw the shit in the bed! Throw it in or I'll blow yer' feckin' head off!"

Justin numbly dropped the items in the back of the truck, his concern for the old man's safety completely forgotten. He chanced a quick look around at all of the chaos still unfolding. More and more people were fighting over trash bags, tape, rolls of plastic and painting masks.

"What's going—" before he could finish the old man struck him on the bridge of the nose with the handgun. Justin dropped to his knees next to the vehicle. His eyes became watery and he clutched his broken nose. The coppery taste of blood spilled into his mouth and he could feel the warm liquid running from between his hands.

He tried standing up on shaking legs and started using the truck for support. He heard the engine roar to life and then toppled over onto the ground as the old man sped away honking his horn. Close to him he could still hear the wails of pain from the two people he injured while trying to protect the old son of a bitch.

Justin groaned as he finally found the energy to stand up, his nose bled freely and his head was spinning from the pain. He stumbled back towards the Jeep, leaving the tire iron where it had fallen. He was almost to Matt's rented vehicle when his cell phone rang.

The sound seemed so foreign to him, so unnatural and not in line at all with what was transpiring in the parking lot. He pulled it from his pocket and through his watery eyes he saw that the call came from Matt. He slid the receiver on and mumbled, "Matt, shith' is gettin' cwazy' out here!"

"Shut up and listen, man! Head over to my dad's basement and grab all the rolls of plastic you can get in the Jeep. He should also have a shitload of tape somewhere around there from when he helped my brother paint, grab all of that too!" Matt's voice was rushed and he sounded out of breath.

"What the hell is going on, Matt? Everyone out here is fighting over anything plast—"

"Fallout rain, man! The fucking Calloway nuclear plant is melting down and radiation is going everywhere. The news is saying to wrap everything up and stay inside. So get the fuck over to my dad's place and then get your ass back to the church, ASAP!" Matt screamed at him and then the phone went dead.

Justin threw the phone in the cab of the Jeep, it bounced off the seat and landed on the floorboard with a dull *thud*. He slammed the door and slowly navigated the vehicle through the parking lot, dodging people as they ran around in a panic, and even though he watched all of this unfold he still couldn't really believe it was happening.

He couldn't believe ANY of this was happening. The mysterious illness that put kids in comas, nuclear fallout rain and, now, looting. It all seemed too unreal and it was hard to take in.

As he turned out of the parking lot he heard gunfire. He gunned the engine and kept his head low. He was surprised at himself and laughed out loud when he realized he was praying under his breath. *As if God's going to do anything to help anyone,* he thought.

Matt snarled as he shoved his cell phone into his pocket. It was useless, it seemed, when he tried to call home to California. His eyes stung from sweat and he used the bottom of his shirt to wipe his face. All around him worried parents were sitting next to their children or, if it was an adult afflicted, a friend would be close at hand.

He had lost sight of Father Murray after the two of them had brought Michael in. He knew that the priest was making rounds with a young woman, Jacqueline he thought her name was, and he was trying to see to the needs of all the people crammed into the building.

Matt gently put a pillow under his friend's head and looked around the small room where most of the adults had been taken. The big man was the youngest of fourteen that were in the church, most of the others were retirement age except for a married couple that was suffering from the mysterious ailment along with their three kids.

After he made sure Michael was as comfortable as possible the former marine carefully navigated his way out of the church, taking extra precaution to not step on any of the comatose victims.

He had found that he was spending as much time outside as he was in, if not more so. Matt looked up towards the sky and at the storm clouds that were approaching as an exasperated sigh slipped from his mouth.

He had tried telling everyone that the fallout was not going to be coming towards them, but the panicked crowd had insisted that they need to put plastic around the windows and then board up the church. Matt was appalled when Father Murray had agreed with them. Most of those who wanted to seal the building had left to try to find materials for the job.

Matt, once he realized his opinion wasn't being listened to, called Justin to let him know where to go and what to do so he wouldn't have to fight a mob of people at the local stores.

The distant rumble of thunder caused worried looks to appear on the faces of those that were gathered outside of the church. Matt couldn't hide a smile when he saw the bloody and bruised faces of those that had went in search of plastic and now stood before him empty handed. *It serves those fuckers right for not listening to me,* he thought.

His smug look quickly faded when Justin pulled onto the grass next to the church. His friend's shirt was covered in dried blood and his nose was bent to the right of his face. Justin opened the door and climbed out of the Jeep on legs that were shaking.

"What the hell?" Matt yelped as he sprinted toward Justin.

"The stuffs inna' backseat," the fallen pastor drunkenly slurred, "I got hit."

Matt shot him a look of disgust when he realized how drunk he was. He grabbed some plastic rolls and stomped toward the church, not saying another word. Justin picked up the last remaining roll of plastic and the bag he had filled with tape. Hanging his head, he followed his friend inside.

Thomas was at the end of his wits with her. She might be great in the sack, but her spoiled and childish outlook on the situation was too much for him to handle right now.

The object of his disdain sat silently across from him at the small table in his kitchen. Jacqueline had her chin resting in her hands while her soft brown eyes continued to look up at him, still silently pleading her request for him to run off with her.

"Where would we go? Where could we go?" he barked at her as his patience finally snapped, "Do you have a private island I don't know about."

The young woman leaned back in her chair and crossed her arms under her small breasts; the white shirt she wore was soaked through with sweat and her bra shown clearly against the wet material.

"You don't have to be rude," her Spanish accent and pouty look made her statement unintentionally sexy, "I only mean to please you. To be away from here so we don't have to keep our love a secret."

Father Murray kept his reaction carefully under control. He smiled at her as he leaned closer to her over the table. He slowly reached out and cupped her face in his hand while he whispered, "I'm sorry, *mi amor*. We can't run off, not yet. We have a duty to help these sick people. After this crisis is over, we can talk more about it."

Jacqueline smiled, nuzzled his hand and then she slowly

started sucking on his fingers while softly moaning. Thomas laughed to himself, despite the strange occurrences and all the stress he was having, this woman was turning him on.

The priest thought about how long he would be able to stay away unnoticed and grinned. He stared at her breasts as they slowly moved in time to her moans. He reached out and roughly pulled her long, dark hair away from her face. She gasped in surprise and then moaned louder as Thomas kissed her deeply.

He stood up and roughly pushed the table out from between them. He unbuttoned his pants and started to pull her face toward his crotch when a loud crashing sound from inside the church caused him to spin toward the door. Jacqueline, who had been leaning forward, jolted back into a sitting position in her chair.

Father Murray quickly began fastening his blue jeans, barely getting them adjusted before there was a loud banging on his door. Before he could open it there were more crashing sounds, like glass breaking. The knocking on his door became more insistent and it sounded like more than one person was waiting outside.

Thomas glanced back towards Jacqueline as he grabbed the door knob, to make sure she was completely covered and decent looking before opening it. Standing in front of him was Michael's friend, Matt and the drunken former pastor, Grady. The fallen pastor had blood all over his shirt and his nose was slightly bent to the right. Matt's face was red and the veins on his neck were standing out.

"You need to get these fucking people under control!" Matt spewed toward the priest, "They're fucking up more shit than they're fixin' and tempers are flaring!"

Father Murray raised his hand to wipe sweat away from his forehead when they all heard yells of joy and excitement coming from the chapel. Justin and Matt looked at each other and as one, turned back and headed down the hallway with the priest and young woman in tow.

When they got near the end of the small hallway they were almost ran over by an excited man wearing a blue button up shirt with fresh blood running down his lip onto his collar. He was smiling as he blurted, "They're waking up! Praise God, they're waking up, Father!"

"What?" Father Murray said as his mind reeled around what the man was saying while he stared at the blood on his shirt.

"The kids, they're waking up! They just started moving around. A bunch of us were arguing, then a few fists flew, and then... then... they just started moving!" the man smiled wider, revealing a few freshly chipped teeth.

"That's great news!" Matt said with a slight tone of sarcasm in his voice, "Now maybe everyone will settle down long enough for us to sort out what—"

"AGHHH!" first one scream, then another, then more echoed from all over the church. The sounds created a symphony of pain and anguish, like an unholy chorus that invaded their ears as they all stood stunned by the sudden change in atmosphere.

The man in the blue shirt sprinted back around the hallway, the sound of his footsteps creating an uneasy beat to the tune of the screams. Jacqueline grabbed onto Father Murray and buried her face in his back while Matt and Justin slowly backed toward the kitchen pushing the other two along.

"Nathan! What are you doing?! Oh, God, Nathan... NOOOO... Glughh!!!" they all heard the man in the blue shirt's scream of pain end in a wet gurgling sound. A sound that came from just up ahead of them and around the corner.

More sounds assaulted them; screams from everywhere, furniture and pews being turned or knocked over in the chapel, and an odd combination of children laughing and crying at the same time.

As they neared the door to the kitchen the smell of blood and feces overpowered their nostrils. From down the hallway they all watched in silent terror as blood began to flow from around the corner, at first just as a trickle then it started coming in larger gouts. Jacqueline could not suppress her scream when, moments later, the man in the blue shirt's head bounced off of the wall and rolled toward them.

"Who shall separate us from the love of Christ? Shall tribulation, or distress, or persecution, or famine, or nakedness, or peril, or sword? As it is written, For thy sake we are killed all the day long; we are accounted as sheep for the slaughter."

- Romans 8:35-36

10

SEE HOW THEY RUN

Owensville, Missouri – Present Day

Sean wrung out the wet towel before placing it on Lewis's forehead. It seemed as if his friend was getting hotter and hotter to the touch and he had to moisten the towel more often to keep him cool.

Sean had only moved from his friend's side a few times since they had brought him in, and each of those times was to check on Michael in the basement. He was glad that Pastor Grady's friend, Matt, was at the church to help. Justin himself appeared barely sober enough to stand, let alone offer assistance to anyone else.

All throughout the church, Sean could hear parent's crying and comforting each other. It didn't seem like such a somber occasion could deteriorate into the bickering and fighting that would suddenly break out when the enormity of it all came crashing down on someone.

"Get away from him, you asshole! Run on back to that fuckin' bitch you left us for!" sobbed Julie.

"I didn't leave him, you crazy whore! I left you!" retorted Mark, his anger finally causing him to raise his voice. "If you weren't such a goddamned bitch, we'd still be married and maybe our son wouldn't be so fucked up!"

More and more sets of eyes were taking notice of the altercation, but the recently divorced couple seemed to be oblivious that they were fast becoming the center of attention in the church.

Sean gritted his teeth and did his best to concentrate on taking care of Lewis while his friend's parents stood arguing over their son's comatose body. He knew that their split had caused his friend a lot of discomfort and he often talked about it to Sean.

"How dare you say this is my fault?!" Julie fumed, her tears falling now more from anger than concern for her son. "I take good care of him! I clothe him and feed him—"

Sean abruptly stood from where he had been kneeling next to Lewis. Mark and Julie stepped back from each other in surprise at the sudden movement he had made. He kept his head down as he walked away from the useless fighting. He rolled his eyes when he began to overhear similar arguments from other adults.

"Watch out, kid! Fuck!"

Sean was jarred from his thoughts when he collided with a pair of men carrying a ladder. One of the men was wearing a red flannel shirt and blue jeans. The other was wearing a dirty white T-shirt and smelled like he had been rolling around in dog shit. Sean bent down and grabbed a large plastic roll that he had knocked out of dog shit's hands as he apologized, "I'm sorry. I didn't see you."

"Well open your damn eyes next time! We have to get this plastic up around these windows or we're all goin' to die!" said dog shit.

"Hey! Watch how you're talkin' to him, shithead, or I'll stuff that ladder so far up your ass you'll be eye to eye with Jesus!" Sean turned to the welcomed sound of Matt's voice, who was standing only a few feet away with Justin at his side.

"Oh, you think so—" the foul smelling man began to say

before his friend interrupted him. "There is enough shit happening outside, guys. Let's not make it hell in here, too!"

Matt and dog shit eyed each other as dog shit was led away by his much calmer companion. Justin looked at Sean and gave him an exaggerated wink. The ridiculous motion, coupled with Justin's bent nose and blood covered shirt, caused Sean to smile at the drunkard.

"Ignore him, bud. I know that asshole from way back and he isn't worth worrying about," Matt said as he continued to watch the pair walk away.

"I'm not worried. Not about him, anyways," Sean said, glancing back toward his friend.

"Lewis is gonna be okay. Justa' wait an' everythin' 'ell work out," mumbled Justin drunkenly to him.

Matt's attention snapped toward Justin and Sean saw a scowl on his face when he spoke, "Man, stop drinking for five damn minutes. Please? Pretty, pretty, please with pussy on top. Just stop drinking for five damn minutes!"

Justin's smile vanished from his face when he regarded his friend. He slowly nodded towards Matt and put his hands deep in his pants pocket. Sean noticed Justin bite his lower lip as Matt closed his eyes and let out a few deep breaths.

"Hey, Matt," Sean said in a low voice, "Is what that guy said true about the plastic on the windows?"

Matt held his voice steady and managed a smile, "I think people are overreacting to the news. I'm not gonna' lie to you, there is a meltdown at a nuclear plant here in Missouri; but the winds are taking the fallout more to the east than in our direction."

"So we're safe?" Sean cocked his head to the side as he looked up at Matt.

Before the older man could reply, a woman let out a wail of pain. Shooting a fast glance toward the sound, Matt's shoulders slumped and his eyes narrowed when he saw a man roughly holding onto her arm and shaking his finger in her face. Matt bounded away in their direction after he slapped Justin on his shoulder.

Sean, not understanding the sudden change in the former Marine's demeanor, watched as he bolted toward Lewis's parents. Justin stumbled after him, using the back of the last row of pews as support.

"Knock it off!" roared Matt as he neared the pair.

The man twisted around to face him while he dropped the woman's arm. Justin recognized the child lying at their feet as Sean's friend, but he couldn't remember the kid's name. The man raised his clenched hands up and bent his knees.

"Mark, 'dis ain't helpin' yer' boy!" Justin slurred drunkenly into the man's face after jumping between him and Matt. "You ta' need ta' come teg' ther' in 'dis time of tragic time!"

There was a moment of silence in the church. It seemed to Matt as though all eyes were on his friend. The man who had been holding the woman slowly let his hands fall to his sides, though they remained curled into fists. He looked back sheepishly at his ex-wife, who was rubbing the fast forming bruise on her arm. She looked at him and extended her middle finger, flipping him off.

Sound returned to the church in a flash. Mark spun back toward Justin and threw a right cross. The drunken man had no chance of stopping it and the blow fell solidly on his left cheek, just below his eye. He crumpled to the floor like one of the many empty and discarded plastic roll containers.

"Oh, hell no!" Matt yelled as launched a brutal kick to Mark's stomach.

The attack knocked the wind out of him and he slumped down to one knee. Matt grabbed the hair on the top of his head with his left hand and raised his opponent's face up just enough to punch him in the nose three times in rapid succession. Matt finished by grabbing the back of his head with both hands and slamming Mark's face into his knee. The man toppled over without making a sound.

Sean stood, open mouthed, at the fury and speed in which Matt had responded to what Mark had done to Justin. Matt looked down at the man and when it became apparent he was out cold he knelt down next to his friend, while still keeping the woman in his sight. She was staring at her ex-husband and her mouth slowly opened and closed a few times.

"Uuuuuhhh…" Justin groaned as Matt pulled him into a sitting position on the carpeted floor. His eyes blinked several times and a large bump was forming on the side of his face.

Matt could hear the woman start to laugh and he shot her a quick glance. He didn't know what expression he had on his face, but whatever it was caused her to stop immediately. She looked back at him, her eyes puffy and red, and did her best to smile.

"Thank you," she said, her voice breaking off at the end as she looked back at her son.

"I got 'it again?" Justin moaned as his senses came back to him.

"Yeah, buddy, you got hit again," Matt managed to chuckle.

Sean watched as the two men began to smile widely at each other and then their bodies started to shake. Justin let out a deep laugh and Matt joined in. The kid didn't understand how they could find anything funny in what had just happened, or about anything that had happened over the last several hours.

Around the trio, other people were involved in their own altercations. One couple was in a heated argument with a single mother who had taken the pillow out from under their daughter's head to use for her son. A young man, barely out of high school, was caught trying to steal a pack of cigarettes from an older man and was now being shoved toward the door. The younger man slipped on a sheet of plastic that had been laid out and tumbled over backwards, knocking over a ladder that was currently in use.

The ladder came crashing down, taking its unfortunate passenger on an unexpected trip that ended when the scared and confused man riding it landed heavily on his side across the back of one of the pews. A loud *snap* erupted when the pew broke in half, spilling those sitting in it onto the floor.

Matt pulled Justin to his feet, all signs of any mirth gone from both of their faces. The pair leaned in close together and spoke in quiet tones that Sean couldn't hear. Justin nodded at Matt and the former Marine motioned for Sean to lean in closer to them.

"We're going to find Father Murray. Go check on Michael, and then stay down there with him. It's getting dangerous in here and we don't want you gettin' hurt!" Matt commanded the boy.

"Okay, but hurry back. I don't like the feeling I'm getting. I can't explain it, but I just think things are going to get worse," Sean said as he hurried off towards the adult's room in the basement.

"That's a good kid, Justin," remarked Matt as the two of them walked in the direction of the kitchen quarters of the church, "Now, let's find this priest so he can settle these fuckin' idiots down!"

The room held an eerie silence compared to the rest of the church. The only real sounds penetrating the walls was the rhythmic breathing of the comatose adults in the room, nine in all, and the tapping of Sean's foot as he impatiently waited for Matt or Justin to come get him.

The room was located just off the main hallway in the basement of the building. Father Murray had insisted that all the children affected by the strange illness remain on the main floor with their parents. However, he allowed the use of the basement for people to store supplies and for adult patients.

Sean leaned against a wall and slid down to come to rest near his friend Michael. The large man still had a wisp of a sad smile plastered on his face, a peaceful expression that both relieved and made Sean jealous.

He thought back to the park and the feeling that had overcame him, he wanted that feeling to come back and stay with him forever. He was still amazed that his legs were completely healed; there weren't even any scars to show he had been injured in the first place!

"What the hell is happening, Mikey?" he asked his unconscious friend, "Did you feel the music, too? Did Lewis?"

Sean leaned closer to the big man and adjusted his pillow. He sat there quietly, listening to breath after breath being taken and exhaled. He pulled his legs close to his body and rested his head against them. He thought about James and Elizabeth, who he hadn't seen since the park was evacuated.

He had not felt this alone in a long time. Before he realized what was happening, he felt wet tears running down his cheeks and his nose was stuffy. He sat in the dimly lit room and let his emotions overcome him.

"Why? Why is this happening?" he croaked out again, between his sobs.

The door flew open and Sean leapt to his feet, doing his best to wipe away tears and snot with the back of his hand. He kept his eyes closed as he tried to compose himself, but opened them when he heard the person at the door laughing at him. When he saw it was dog shit, his initial embarrassment at being caught crying and laughed at was replaced by anger.

His arms started to shake and he rocked back and forth on his feet as he yelled, "Stop laughing at me, asshole!"

"Oh, now what's wrong, crybaby?" dog shit mocked him, "Your friends not here to keep people from picking on you?"

Sean glared at him as another round of laughter erupted from the smelly man, "You better run and tell them that the bad man is making fun of you!"

Sean roared and charged dog shit, the laughing stopped as he used all of his weight and momentum to push his shoulder as hard as he could into the man's stomach.

"Oooof!" was the only sound he could make as the kid hit him.

Dog shit was barreled onto the ground and Sean managed to stay on top of him. He swung wildly at the man's face and the wide mouthed look of surprise only fueled him onward to swing even harder.

He landed five or six hard hits on dog shit before the stronger man bucked him off. Sean landed hard on his right knee and when he tried to stand his leg gave out. He landed on his side and dog shit kicked him in the small of his back.

"You little cocksucker! I'm going to fucking kill you!" screamed dog shit, launching snot and blood from his ruined nose onto the back of Sean's neck.

"You better kill me, asshole!" Sean screamed back at the man as he scurried away, still trying to regain his footing.

"You can bet on that!" the man mumbled as he pulled a knife from his pocket.

"Really? Really, you fucking coward? You're going to use a knife on a kid?" Sean laughed at the absurdity of the situation.

"Nah, I'm going to use this knife on the Goddamned prick that broke my nose!" dog shit yelled as he lunged at Sean.

Sean jumped back and raised his arms up to cover his torso, something he had read about doing in case an opponent had a knife. Dog shit only made it a few steps before a hand grabbed his ankle and yanked him off of his feet. He let go of his knife to catch his fall and the weapon bounced a few feet out of his reach.

Sean let out a yelp of excitement when he saw Michael sit up, his hand still firmly holding dog shit by the ankle. "Mikey! Man, you picked the right time to wake up!"

"Let go of me you fucking retard!" wailed dog shit as he tried to crawl toward his knife.

"Don't do it, Mikey! He said he was going to—" Sean's words died in his throat when Michael turned his head toward him. His friends once blue eyes were black as tar and had a nightmarish pinpoint of red in the center of the pupils. His skin was ashen grey and his hands were twisted, appearing claw-like. He opened his mouth wide, revealing teeth that looked more like thick needles and purplish gums that bled.

Michael lashed out with his other hand and grasped dog shit's foot. Sean heard a loud *snap* as the bone was torn from its socket. Dog shit let out a yell so strong and pitiful that Sean felt his legs go weak. The poor man's leg was barely being held onto his pelvis.

The creature that once was Michael brought the leg up to its waiting maw and bit through the blue jeans into the soft flesh underneath. Blood spurted over the beast's face as it ripped a chunk of meat away from the leg, exposing the bones.

Dog shit's mouth flew open and he made whimpering sounds, but for some reason a scream wouldn't come out. He looked at Sean and then at the creature that was eating him. He reached out to Sean…

Another hand snaked out and clutched dog shit's wrist. Sean gasped when he saw that it was an old woman, her eyes and teeth just as hellish looking as Michael's. She pulled herself closer to him and cackled madly just before biting his thumb off.

"Help me!" Dog shit finally managed to scream, blood

poured from his leg and squirted from his mangled hand as he struggled against Michael's hold on him.

Sean numbly backed toward the open door. All around him eyes were opening and limbs were starting to come to life. Eyes that once might have held kindness in their gaze now burned with hate and hunger.

Sean fought against his fear and managed to keep his screams bottled up in his chest as he witnessed the monsters converge on dog shit. Any opening that could be found was quickly filled with a bite and the ripping away of a chunk of his skin and muscle.

He stumbled out into the hallway and shut the door. He stood there for a few horrible seconds and listened to the slurping sounds of the creatures feeding before he turned and ran for the staircase that led upstairs into the chapel.

Sean yanked his arm back just before his hand could rest on the knob when the sounds assailed him. Still shaking, he put his ear against the thick wooden door hoping things would be clearer.

Incoherent screams and pleas created a hellish chorus in the chapel. There was another sound that Sean couldn't quite make out, something completely foreign against the background of the nightmare that was going on. It almost sounded like children laughing.

His mind reeled, trying to make sense of what was happening. He was surprised when he felt his hand close around the door knob, an act that had been completely unconscious on his part. He pulled his ear away from the door and stood as tall as he could.

Sean took several deep breaths as he slowly began to turn the handle. His hand didn't want to respond to his commands to open the door and a part of his brain, the primal survivalist, screamed at him to stop. Sean's deep breathing turned into fast pants as he struggled with the inner battle he was holding with himself.

EDWARD GEHLERT

With tears streaming down his face, he snatched his hand away from the door and pounded his fist against the brick wall of the staircase in frustration. His body shook with sobs and the pain in his hand, created by his assault on the wall, only fueled more wild strikes.

The screams from the other side of the door became more intense and were mixed with the screeching sound of breaking glass and the cracking of wood. Sean finally accepted the reality of what was happening. The children had woken up. Or at least their bodies had awakened, along with something dark and sinister.

He thought of the creature downstairs that once was Michael. Michael, a man so gentle and caring, was now replaced with something—

A shudder suddenly ran through Sean's body. He turned sharply, facing the door again, and firmly grasped the handle. He could feel that behind him, at the bottom of the stairs, hungry eyes were staring up at him.

He took a deep breath and when he heard heavy stomps rushing up the staircase he pushed the door open and lunged into the chapel. As he turned to slam the door, he saw Michael at the head of a mob of the creatures. His face and shirt was covered in dog shit's blood. His mouth was open, revealing the needle like teeth that still had chunks of human meat wedged between them. The rest of the creatures were also covered in varying degrees of blood and gore, with one even still gnawing at the last pieces of flesh on what appeared to be a leg bone.

Sean slammed the door with as much force as his terror could summon and felt a moment of triumph when he heard all of the beasts running into each other. He slid the dead bolt closed and spun around.

The sounds he had heard from behind the relative safety of the heavy oaken door did not do the scene before him any justice. The children had woken up hungry. The carpet in the chapel was soaked with blood and other fluids, as were the pews and altar. Many of the little beasts had already claimed their victims and were noisily munching on their meals.

Sean bolted toward the apartment section of the church; vaulting over pews and other furniture that was in his way.

As he ran, he saw the monster that once was Lewis. His friend had his mother face down and was cackling as he slammed her head onto the ground again and again until it caved in.

In horror, he watched as Lewis pulled a huge handful of her brains to his mouth and began chewing. He couldn't look away, even as he ran, he couldn't look away from the grisly scene. For one terrible moment their eyes met. The creature smiled at him and waved.

Luckily, or by some divine favor, he had a clear path to the hallway that led to the kitchen of the church. He pumped his legs as hard as he could. Hate filled eyes tracked his movements from all across the room as he ran, while salivating mouths with sharp fangs feasted on the flesh of their parents.

A younger woman sprinted past his field of vision. Her eyes were wide and unblinking as blood spurted from a jagged gash in her throat. Her arms flailed at her back where a small girl, maybe three or four years old, was ripping away chunks of her flesh with its mouth while tearing at her hair with its free hands. The woman slammed blindly into the altar and crumpled atop it without making a sound.

The child-beast cooed happily as it began to peel chunks of quivering flesh from its mother and place them in its maw. The beast looked up and hissed loudly at the cross hanging on the wall behind the altar. It tore an ear off the unfortunate lady and threw it at the holy symbol while jumping to the ground. With an impossible strength, it dragged the woman's body off the altar and headed toward a corner of the room.

Sean rounded the corner to the hallway and tripped over the body of a man wearing a blue buttoned up shirt. Sean hurtled forward, landing heavily on the carpet, and came face to face with a decapitated head that was missing its nose and left eye.

He shuffled backwards on his hands and knees to get away from the gruesome object, accidently kicking the corpse. He shuffled to the side and dared a look at what he had struck; part of the man's arm had been gnawed on. His stomach tightened up as he violently expelled his last meal. The vomit mingled with the blood surrounding the headless corpse and steam rose up from the putrid mixture.

Sean wiped his hand across his mouth and looked past the

head. At the end of the hallway the door to the kitchen was open. Inside he could see that the refrigerator was knocked on its side and the table had been overturned. Blood was everywhere in the small room.

He willed himself to stand and continue his run. As he entered the kitchen he silently closed the door and locked it. The boy rested his back against the door and started to shake all over. He awkwardly walked over to the sink and numbly turned on the cold water.

He splashed the liquid on his face and rinsed his mouth out. He stuck his head under the faucet and cupped his hands to drink while at the same time letting the cold water cascade over his head.

A guttural snarl from the pantry made Sean jerk his head up, spraying water everywhere around the sink. He grabbed a large knife from the dish drainer and crept toward the snarls. He paused when the sounds turned to crunching and he heard a low pitiful moan accompanying it.

Whatever was around the corner, it was between him and the door leading outside to the garden, to freedom. He hefted the knife and held it out in front of him. His muscles tensed and, before his courage could fail him, he jumped around the corner into the living room. His leap interrupted the meal of one of the hellish creatures, a creature that was now staring at him.

"Be alert and of sober mind. Your enemy the devil prowls around like a roaring lion looking for someone to devour. Resist him, standing firm in the faith, because you know that the family of believers throughout the world is undergoing the same kind of sufferings."

- 1 Peter 5:8-9

11

THE MONKEY CHASED THE WEASEL

Jacqueline's scream suddenly caught in her throat, as the body the head was once attached to slammed violently against the hallway wall. The impact created a fountain of blood to be forced out of the body and the sticky fluid washed over the ceiling and floor.

The body was still twisting and jerking as it landed. It flopped a few more times and finally came to rest in the middle of the hallway. Thick blood continued to pump from the destroyed arteries in the neck, creating a coppery smelling pool that was fast spreading toward the group.

Matt's muscles tensed. Next to him, Justin stood open mouthed at the scene and swayed on his feet. Matt couldn't tell if the movement was caused by the events surrounding them or the copious amounts of vodka his friend had ingested. Behind him, he heard muffled sobs coming from the young woman and a sudden sharp intake of breath by the priest.

A small boy, maybe seven or eight years old, rounded the

corner. The original color of his shirt was undistinguishable under the saturation of blood coating his body. Matt took a few quick steps toward the child but suddenly stopped—

The boy giggled with delight and roughly bit into the right arm of the corpse, revealing razor sharp teeth to tear away skin. The child swiftly swallowed and moved in for more.

Jacqueline's voice miraculously returned at that moment and she wailed, "God! No! No! No! God, no!"

The creature's attention shifted to the group. Its eyes, black as night with an unholy reddish glow in the pupils, stared at them intently. It chewed slowly, opening its mouth wide as if to show what fate awaited those that fell to its hunger. It giggled some more, spewing small pieces of its meal onto the carpet.

Matt slowly walked backwards with his arms at his sides. He waved behind him toward his friend, hoping that Justin was coherent enough to understand that he wanted him to head toward the kitchen.

Jacqueline's wailing become muffled as Father Murray turned her around and clamped a hand over her mouth. The priest felt her body begin to go limp. He twisted her arm until she yelped painfully. He felt strength returning to her body so he eased up the pressure. Thomas forcefully whispered in her ear, "Shut the fuck up!"

The vehemence in his tone was like a physical slap across her face. Her body became more rigid in his grasp and she seemed to have more control over her movements. Thomas let her go and gave her a gentle, but firm, push toward the open door of the kitchen.

The woman stumbled forward. Father Murray, his body only inches from hers, moved with carefully measured steps. Justin retreated backwards with his hands on the wall for support, his control over his body clouded from the booze.

Matt locked stares with the child-fiend as he also moved towards the kitchen. The beast dropped the arm it had been feasting on and stalked toward the group. It slowed as it neared the severed head.

Dull eyes stared vacantly up at the monster. The tongue lolled out of the heads mouth and saliva slowly dripped from it. The creature reached down and picked it up by the hair. It held the gruesome trophy out in front of it toward Matt. Wickedly sharp teeth suddenly sank into the face and ripped the nose off.

A low growl came from deep in the monster's chest as it stared at Matt. It held up its left hand, which now more resembled a claw with sharp talons instead of nails, and with one swift motion gouged an eye from the skull.

Matt's vision narrowed. All he could see was the eyeball, tauntingly being wiggled on the end of one of the talons. In what seemed like slow motion to him, the monster brought it up to its mouth. Almost playfully, it sucked the organ off of its finger and bit down. Wet smacking sounds now mingled with contented growls from the beast.

"Move it!" the priest's voice sounded from behind, pulling Matt out of the semi-trance he was in.

The former Marine cursed himself under his breath. He had stopped moving at some point and was only about ten feet from the beast, which had now slumped close to the ground and was shuffling forward. Its black eyes, with those hellish red spots, locked right on him.

"Justin, when I turn around. make sure you get your ass on the other side of that door," Matt said, emphasizing each word.

"What ya' thinkin', man?" slurred Justin.

"I'm thinking, when I turn around, you get your ass on the other side of that door. NOW!" Matt yelled as he spun toward the kitchen.

The sudden movement spurred the rest of the small group to burst into a flurry of action. Father Murray roughly shoved Jacqueline the rest of the way into the kitchen. She fell over the edge of the table, causing the cheap light wooden furniture to topple over. The priest grabbed her arm as he ran by, roughly trying to jerk her to her feet. Justin, who had already began turning around when Matt first commanded him to get into the kitchen, sprung forward.

The drunken man gave the overturned table too wide of a berth and crashed into the refrigerator. His momentum hurled him back, but he was able to grab onto the door latch of the appliance. His weight, aided by the power of gravity dragging him down, upset the balance of the machine and it came crashing down; only narrowly missing his right leg.

Matt rocketed toward the doorway, witnessing the chaos unfold in front of him. His chest seemed to freeze when the beast behind him wailed. It sounded like a child who had been grievously injured. He ignored the urge to look behind him, somehow knowing that's what the monsters intention was.

As Matt sprinted past the threshold of the door, searing pain erupted from his right shoulder as he felt claws dig into his flesh. Without thinking, he grabbed the bestial appendage and pulled forward as hard as he could while ducking into a roll.

Justin, who had somehow managed to get to his feet with lightning speed, watched in awe as his friend hurled the creature off of his back. The intensity of the momentum carried the monster into the kitchen, which smacked loudly against the wall where the refrigerator had been.

The creature emitted a shrieking sob and shuffled around on top of the overturned appliance, trying to regain its footing. Father Murray managed to pull Jacqueline onto one knee before the hell-child lashed out.

Jacqueline's eyes widened in pain and surprise when the talon's of the creature's hand penetrated the muscles just below her right elbow. She saw blood, her blood, splash across Thomas' face as the priest recoiled in horror.

She felt sharp pressure deep in her right arm. Suddenly it became very cold then turned numb when she heard a loud snapping sound. She reached out for her lover and stared dumbfounded when she realized that her right arm and been ripped away at her elbow. She started to scream incoherently when the direness of her situation crept into her brain.

Father Murray quickly began to back away from the young woman as blood spurted from the hellish amputation, covering the front of him. His stomach felt tight as he helplessly watched the child hungrily chomp down on Jacqueline's severed arm.

Matt, after recovering from his roll, was on his feet next to Justin. The former Marine took in the scene before him and grabbed his friend. He shouted, "Out the back!"

Justin started to move toward the injured woman as the

priest ran toward the door leading to an outside patio. Matt tightened his grip on the drunk and pleaded, "Bud, she's a goner and we'll be too if we stay here!"

Justin allowed himself to be pushed toward the door by Matt. Both of them following the concrete path Father Murray set out on. It took everything for Matt not to turn around when he heard the young woman scream out, "Help me!"

In answer to her plea, Matt shut the door. In front of him he could hear wracking sobs coming from Justin. For a moment, but just a short one, he felt bad about leaving the woman behind. He looked at his friend and felt anger flow through him at how Justin was going to risk his life for that girl. Matt shook away the anger and made a promise to himself that he would get back to his wife, no matter what he had to do.

Her hopes for survival slammed shut just as loudly as the door through which Father Murray had fled with the other two men. Behind her she could hear the monster noisily feasting on her arm.

Jacqueline felt weak and cold. She was shivering violently and her remaining limbs didn't want to cooperate with her wishes. She slumped to the floor on her left side and, using her remaining arm, slowly crawled around the corner toward the pantry.

The beast, still sitting on the overturned refrigerator, stopped chewing for a few seconds and watched her as she struggled to move. It slid off the appliance and grabbed her by her right foot.

Jacqueline suddenly found herself on her back as she was roughly turned over. She saw that the beast still clutched her arm in its left hand and was now holding her foot up to its face with the other.

The child sniffed her foot a few times and seemed to be examining her shoe. She jerked her leg with as much force as she could muster and it came out of the monsters grasp. The beast hissed at her and smacked her across the face with her own severed arm.

She whimpered pitifully. The monster laughed at the noises she made and smacked her again with the severed appendage. Another moan issued from Jacqueline. The sound threw the beast into a cackling fit. With squeals of delight, the monster repeatedly beat the helpless woman with his gruesome weapon as she slowly crawled along the floor.

The young woman managed to flip over on her stomach. She continued her crawling as best as she could, although now she was feeling lightheaded and colder than she could ever remember being before.

She hadn't been attacked again since she had turned over. Her mind was screaming out in fear at her to look and see what the monster was doing. She continued her slow crawl and fought against the darkness that was creeping in, threatening to drag her into oblivion.

The silence of the kitchen was suddenly broken by the sound of water running in the sink. The child-beast stared in the direction of the commotion and absently ripped and chewed pieces of meat from the severed leg it was still holding.

Jacqueline glanced behind her through eyes that were fast dimming. Her movement caused the creature to snarl at her. She began to whimper more when it bit into her severed leg with enough force to crunch into the bone. Tears rolled down her face as she watched its greedy tongue licking at her marrow.

She felt a moment of relief when the beast went rigid as Sean jumped from around the corner. Then she knew only darkness.

Sean gritted his teeth and fought to keep his arms from shaking. He saw Jacqueline laying on her stomach with her eyes staring up at him. For a moment he thought about Miss Hevener, then his mind sped up as the monster lunged at him.

He hastily took a step to his right and leaned back as the beast swung a severed and broken arm at him. Without thinking, he stepped in as the appendage whizzed past and brought the knife up. The blade entered the creatures head through its lower jaw and was wrenched away from his grasp as the beast suddenly crumpled.

Sean stared down at the unmoving bodies at his feet. The brutality of the monsters feeding was evident by the whelps on Jacqueline's face, and by the condition of her severed arm. Sean slowly knelt down next to the creature and grabbed the hilt of the knife with both hands and gave it a sharp jerk.

Blood spurted from the wound as the knife came free, accompanied by a slurping sound. Sean stared in fascination at the warm sticky fluid that was now covering both of his hands. It looked like blood, but the smell… The smell reminded him of burnt matchsticks.

Sean stood up and made his way back into the kitchen. He dropped the knife in the sink and turned on the water. He began vigorously scrubbing his hands. Hot water flowed over his fingers as he stared at the blood being washed away. Steam rose from the sink as Sean continued to roughly wash his hands.

His face was wet from a combination of the steam and tears he couldn't control. He could hear screams coming from the church. Each wail causing him to scrub harder and harder on his hands, causing them to become raw, as more sobs escaped him. Blood pounded in his ears, adding a macabre beat to the screams that continued from horrified parents in the chapel.

Sean stepped away from the sink after grabbing a hand towel. He dried his hands and absently looked around the kitchen. His eyes locked onto the large knife he had used to kill Phillip.

Phillip… The kid-turned-monster's name was Phillip! Sean was suddenly wracked with a wave of guilt. He remembered seeing the kid on the school bus and even had bought some popcorn from him earlier in the year to support the Boy Scout troop he was in.

Sean retrieved the knife from the sink and dried it with the hand towel as he opened the door leading to the outside patio. Each step he took down the concrete path grew faster than the last, until he was running. The continuing screams he heard echoing inside the church fueled the strength and purpose in each of his strides. He had to find Elizabeth. He had to find

James. After that, they could look for Justin, Matt and Father Murray.

Sean ran toward the church's garage where he kept his bicycle and camping gear. He quickly pulled his keys from his pocket and unlocked the padlock holding the door shut. Turning on the light felt uncomfortable for him so he stood in the darkness. When lightning flashed through the windows he moved.

It took him a few moments to navigate through some of the clutter, but he finally breathed a sigh of relief when he pushed his bike out of the garage after he put on his backpack. He adjusted the straps on his pack and started riding his bike toward Elizabeth's house, nine blocks away.

As Sean rode away from the church, the screech of shattering glass from behind him caused him to turn his bike around. One of the heavy stained glass windows on the side of the church had been shattered from the inside.

When Sean saw Michael climbing out of the destroyed window, he held his breath in the hope that his friend was back to normal. He let the air out of his lungs in a defeated sigh when he saw red orbs staring back at him from a twisted version of Michael's face.

The beast began running toward him, howling like an animal, and Sean pumped his legs as fast as he could to outdistance the monster. The only way he could tell if he was getting away was from the sounds of those howls. It seemed as if they kept getting closer and closer to him. He peddled as hard as he could and tried to ignore the death that was fast beating down upon him. Ahead of him, a dog that was chained to a post was barking and snarling at him as he approached.

The dog saved his life. The beast behind him must have thought it would be an easier meal to catch. Sean continued to stare straight ahead when he heard the dog yelping in pain. A yapping that was suddenly cut short by the sharp *crack* of its head being ripped away from its shoulders.

"For we do not wrestle against flesh and blood, but against the rulers, against the authorities, against the cosmic powers over this present darkness, against the spiritual forces of evil in the heavenly places."

- Ephesians 6:12

GIRLS AND BOYS, COME OUT TO PLAY...

His breathing came in slow measured breaths as he surveyed the scene in front of Elizabeth's house. From his concealment under the bush in the corner of her neighbor's yard, he slowly unscrewed the cap of the canteen he was holding.

Moving as quietly as possible, James took a small sip from the container to wet his dry mouth as he continued to watch the carnage unfolding. It was hard to swallow the water through the lump in his throat.

He couldn't believe there was an actual zombie apocalypse happening. He was sure that people would call it something else, blame it on a virus, or just try to write it off as cosmic rays or some such shit. But, James knew it was what it was; a God-damned ZOMBIE apocalypse.

Since he had fled his house he had been chased by former friends and classmates. He was grateful that, so far, he had only been scratched and not bitten. He knew that a bite would turn him into one of the creatures. He knew that, just as he knew it was a zombie apocalypse… It just made sense somehow to him.

His initial plan had been to try to round up his Z.O.D. group, but all of them had been afflicted with it and turned into the damnable monsters! Except for Sean. He was certain his friend was okay and would be making his way to Elizabeth's house, as he had done.

Contemplating what he had just seen in her front yard though, he didn't know if she was even still alive. He risked another look from beneath the bush and shook his head in frustration. On the lawn, three of the child-beasts were hissing at a much larger monster.

James thought he recognized it as once being the man who ran the community outreach program in town. This creature, however, only somewhat still resembled a human at all. It was at least seven feet tall, with grubby greyish skin, and huge almost comical muscles.

The beast stomped around the yard, ripping huge chunks of its own flesh away. Roars issued from the monster with each handful it slung to the ground. James gritted his teeth against the sound but could not look away from what was occurring. It appeared that the wounds the beast was inflicting on itself were healing at an amazing rate, seeming to fill in as fast as new handfuls were torn away.

The smaller creatures would charge in and scoop up the discarded flesh and greedily gobble it down. Each time one of them would get too close, the larger one would lash out with a punch or a kick. James was astounded at the strength of the creature when a kick sent one of the little ones sailing across the street to crash through the second floor window of an unfortunate house.

The two remaining smaller ones quickly scuttled away from the larger beast, wailing like babies. James had never heard such a pitiful sound in his life. He was almost grateful when human screams cut through the monsters shrill noises.

The screams came from the house across the street. The house the smaller creature was punted into. James felt his stomach lurch again when three teenagers, two girls and a boy a little older than him, came running out the front door.

The two small monster's screams suddenly sounded cheerful as they bounded toward the panicked trio. The group turned as one and sprinted off down the street toward the center of town, screaming as loudly as they could. The child-beasts leapt in unison, seeming to easily clear the fifteen or so feet to their target, and landed on top of the boy.

Their weight bore him to the ground. His screams of fear quickly shifted to yells of pain as they began to tear into him with claws and teeth. Even from his distant vantage point, James could see pieces of the kid being strewn violently about his body.

The girls didn't even look behind them. They barreled away as fast as they could. James covered his ears as the larger monster let out its loudest roar yet. The only thing he could compare it to was the sound of all the tools running in his dad's body shop. The gigantic creature sped off after the girls.

Everything was too overwhelming for James. These were not just *any* zombies... They were *super* zombies! He could only admire, and cringe in horror, at the power behind each step of the brute as it chased after the girls. In what seemed like only a few great strides it was right behind them.

The creature delivered a vicious backhand to the girl on the right. The force of the blow sent her flying into the air. Her screams took on an even more urgent tone as her brain suddenly understood the pain that was about to be inflicted on it. Her yell was cut off when she slammed into a brick chimney on the roof of a neighboring house. Her body went limp as her head exploded against the unyielding brickwork. James watched as her corpse slid down the shingles and fell softly on the lawn.

The huge monster seized the remaining girl by her head. One of its monstrous hands easily cupped her skull, muffling her terrified screams. Her legs continued to try to flee as the monster lifted her off the ground and bit into her shoulder, it's teeth ripping through skin and bone with equal ease.

James couldn't wait any longer. With the creatures distracted he sprinted from his concealment towards Elizabeth's front door. *What if the door's locked?!* Screamed a panicked thought in his head. The thought was banished as fast as it came to him when the door flew open and he saw Elizabeth on the other side, unharmed.

He rocketed into the house and collapsed shaking on a plush, oversized green chair. Elizabeth shut the door and slid the deadbolt closed. James watched her from the chair as she turned around and stared at him through tear stained eyes.

"I didn't know what to do," she began, "My mom and dad left to get my uncle and ain't back yet. I saw those... those... THINGS and I didn't know what to do!"

James slowly stood up and embraced her in an awkward hug. He felt her tense up at first then she just seemed to melt into him. Her body shook as more tears began to form and James found himself fighting against the sudden onslaught of emotion he was feeling.

He thought about Sean and the monsters that were roaming the streets. He felt sick when he thought of the possibility that Lewis, or the beast that he most likely turned into, had killed and eaten him.

He looked down at Elizabeth, who was now staring at him through those brown doe-eyes, and felt lost. He had formulated a simple, yet effective, plan; a plan that should have been easy to pull off and expand upon. Now though... James shook his head and whispered, "How long do we wait here? For your parents, for Sean, for anyone? How long do we wait here?"

Elizabeth was taken aback by the question. The thought of leaving her house had never entered her mind! She felt safe here. She didn't want to face the hell that was happening outside, she just wasn't prepared! She had no idea where they could even go for safety. Was there anywhere still safe?

James could see her struggling for an answer. He could see that she had just as much indecision in her as he did. He wished Sean was with him. He wished Lewis was with him. He wished that Clyde was...

"We can head to Zelch Farms. Clyde has all kinds of supplies there and I know that man can help us!" he blurted out.

"What about Sean?" she asked, "Don't you think he'd come here?"

"If, and I know this is shitty to say, but if he's still alive that would be the next place he would head to," James stated, his voice full of confidence.

"Can we give him just a little more ti—"

The window next to the oversized plush chair exploded inward with a screech of shattering glass as one of the smaller beasts invaded the house. The monsters mad cackling and sudden appearance sent Elizabeth into a screaming fit. James was roughly shoved to the ground by the beast, which then turned towards the hysterical girl.

Elizabeth spun on her heels and blindly ran for the kitchen. The creature gave chase and snatched a handful of her hair. The beast yanked viciously, driving her onto her back on the hardwood floor.

The force of the impact knocked the air from her lungs and she struggled for breath; all the while her head screaming out in pain. The monster wasted no time in climbing on top of her. She flailed pathetically, trying to force the creature off her. With lightning speed, it pinned her arms to the floor above her head. She closed her eyes as it leaned in, not wanting to see its evil eyes and fang filled mouth. She could feel the heat from its breath on her face and neck. Even though she could barely draw breath, the stench coming from the creature's mouth was horrid and caused her to turn her head to the side.

She felt hot, sticky saliva splash on her chin and then the weight of the monster was suddenly gone. She opened her eyes when the crashing sound of furniture being destroyed echoed through the living room, along with snarls and screeches from the beast.

She struggled to sit up when she realized that James was fighting for his life against the monster. She collapsed again to the floor in fear when she heard the roar of the larger enraged monster outside, its calls blending with the hissing of several smaller sinister voices. A much louder roar answered the first and she felt herself starting to lose consciousness…

"Help me!" yelled James, snapping her awake. She looked in the direction of his voice and watched as he used a couch cushion to keep the monster's claws and fangs from him.

Elizabeth used the couch to pull herself to her feet. She grabbed the lamp off of the end table closest to her and rushed up behind the beast. It abruptly twisted about to face her when she was close enough to swing her makeshift weapon. She had barely managed to raise the lamp when she was punched in the jaw. Her legs buckled and fell out from underneath her as she stumbled over backwards, landing in a daze.

"Elizabeth!" James yelled as he saw her crumple to the floor.

He kicked the small beast in the back to get its attention before it could do anymore damage to his friend. His attack worked and the child-beast whirled on him in a flurry of slashes and small jumps, all the while hissing. James backed away from where Elizabeth was struggling to regain her senses. He had a momentary feeling of triumph when he led the beast into the kitchen and spotted a heavy looking meat tenderizing hammer on the counter. A loud banging on the back door forced his hand. He had to get some kind of weapon before more of the beasts surged in. As a sudden and violent battering against the door shook its frame, he made a grab for the utensil.

As if reading his mind, the creature moved toward it at the same moment. Instead of grasping a weapon in his hand, James was now doing his best to hold the monsters arms to keep them from slashing him. It continued to push and pull against him, snapping at him with needle-like fangs as it tried to free itself.

James knew he couldn't hold it for long. He chanced a look into the living room to see if Elizabeth was up yet. His heart sank when he saw her unmoving legs sprawled out from behind the couch. In that one moment of distraction, the monster used all of the strength in its legs to jump backwards.

The force pulled James forward and he found himself falling. He scrambled onto his back when he hit the off-white tile of the kitchen floor. James was fast. He was one of the fastest kids in his karate class and he had a lot of trophies from competitions to prove it. But, as fast as he was, the monster was the quicker of the two.

As James was on his back, the creature leapt on his chest and pinned his arms above his head. The hellish red of the monsters eyes seemed to blaze with an inner fire as it leaned in toward him. Its maw opened wide, eagerly waiting for a bite of his flesh. This was the same predicament from which he had just saved Elizabeth. He doubted she was currently in any condition to return the favor.

Small pools of water from the storm had formed on the terrain. Steam rose up from the blacktop, creating a translucent fog that slowly danced along the surface in the wind. The crisp, clean smell of the rain created the illusion of a peaceful night.

Sean kept a steady rhythm on his bicycle while keeping an eye out for more monsters lurking in the streets. He hadn't seen any as he peddled towards Elizabeth's house, but he could hear screams. They seemed to come from everywhere around him.

The town was actually alive with all kinds of sounds. Most of them, however, were a reminder of the hell that had been unleashed. Screams of pain barely overpowered the cackling of the beasts. Sean much preferred to hear the sounds of the screams. They at least were human.

His sharp eyes caught sudden movement up ahead. He turned his bike into a small alley on the side of the street and stared intently down the block. There it was again… Only this time he could see the outline of small, hunched creatures shambling over fences and shuffling around on lawns.

They moved low to the ground, and it appeared as if they were sniffing their new territory like dogs. A small pack of the creatures gathered on the side of a fresh cut lawn. They ambled about for a few moments until one of their numbers suddenly rushed the house. The rest scurried after it, each one leaping up to the top of the roof. Loud *thumps* sounded in the night, attracting the attention of more of the beasts.

The new additions to the hell-pack ignored the roof and burst through the windows on the first floor. Panicked yells emitted from the home. Sean watched as a second floor window was opened by an older woman. The look of terror on her face as she started to climb out was something he would never forget. She was immediately plucked up onto the roof by some of the creatures. Her screams flooded the neighborhood as her flesh was torn from her and deposited into hungry mouths.

He peddled down the alley away from the gristly scene. More screams were coming from the house now. He knew there was nothing he could do to save them. He looked back to make sure he wasn't being followed by any of the monsters then concentrated on navigating the darkened alleyway.

The handlebars of his bike were suddenly wrenched hard to the right as the front tire shifted violently. He ran into a privacy fence and was knocked off his seat. He lay on the ground, shaken a bit but not hurt. In the low-light, Sean spied what had caused his wreck. He had missed seeing an old discarded shovel in the middle of the alley. His front tire must have clipped it.

He stood up and retrieved his bike. As soon as he saw the damage his heart sank in his chest. The wheel was bent. Without thinking he picked up his bike and hurled it over the privacy fence. His ears burned and he tasted blood in his mouth. His arms were shaking from frustration and he felt angry tears forming in his eyes.

He channeled as much of his fury as he could to propel him through the alley. His annoyance with the destruction of his tire faded when he saw a bike, similar to his, leaning against a chain-link fence. He realized, with an overwhelming sadness, that most bikes would be unclaimed. Their previous owners now transformed into something unholy, more interested in murder and mayhem than in laughing with friends and riding through the streets on a nice summer night.

With his head low, he pulled the bike away from the fence. Something underneath it stopped him cold. He felt his face flush and he sucked in a gasp of air when he recognized it. There, piled up on the ground next to the fence, was a small pile of rocks with sticks jutting out from between the stones.

His mind jumped back seven years. He remembered the last day he spent with his mom and brother. He remembered the walk along the riverbank. He also remembered the strange pile of rocks and sticks along with the smiling old man.

Moving as if in a dream; he fell to the ground on his knees and began tearing apart the small cairn. Halfway into the pile, he found a rectangular plastic case about four inches high. He brushed more of the dirt and debris off of it and found the clasps that held it shut. He clicked them open and bit his lower lip when he saw what the mysterious case held. A pistol.

He could barely make out *Ruger* on the hand grip as he examined it. Hefting the weapon for a closer view, he noticed a magazine was inserted. He popped it out. Judging by its weight he estimated it to be full. He put the magazine back into the pistol and grabbed the remaining three he saw in the case, all loaded. He tucked the weapon into his waistband at the small of his back and placed the magazines in his pants pockets.

He hopped on the bike and cycled towards Elizabeth's house, this time using the alleyway and the darkness for concealment. *I have to follow the piles,* he thought. He didn't have any logical explanation for the thought. He just knew it was something he had to do, even if he didn't know where to look for them.

As he neared his destination he saw a small mob of the little beasts. They had a much larger and more fearsome creature in their midst. The thing was at least seven feet tall. Sean had seen numerous muscle magazines before. The monster in front of his eyes would easily put any of their cover models to shame.

The massive beast was stomping around the yard to a chorus of hisses being thrown its way from the littler ones. Occasionally it would lash out at the smaller monsters if they got too close, but otherwise it ignored them and concentrated on battering at the ground with its hands and feet.

Sean skirted the edge of yards and tried his best to stay in the shadows as he maneuvered his way toward the house. The closer he crept, the more creatures seemed to appear on the lawn. He knew it was his imagination, but he kept counting the beasts as he moved.

With legs shaking, he ran the remaining few yards to the side of Elizabeth's house. He tried to calm down and catch his breath as his mind raced for an idea on how to enter the dwelling unnoticed by the creatures.

A crashing sound, mingled with horrified screams, came from inside the house. He dared a look through the window above him. His heart froze as he watched Elizabeth being roughly slammed to the floor by one of the small creatures. He almost screamed when the monster climbed on top of her and snapped at her face. The scream turned into a cheer when James tackled her assailant, sending both of them sprawling across the floor.

Another loud roar from the front lawn split the night, accompanied by a round of hissing. Sean ignored it and headed toward the back door as fast as he could. A deeper roar issued and he skidded to a halt. Looking behind him, he gasped at what had become of Michael.

His friend-turned-monster stood across the street and stared intently at the front of the house. He was now taller than anything alive Sean had ever seen. The only feature recognizable from before the change was his square jawline. The creature crested at least ten feet tall with muscles rippling all over its body. Each movement it made seemed to flex all of them at once, giving the beast an over exaggerated gait. Greyish skin fell from its body as it strode toward the house, only to be replaced a few steps later.

"Help me!" he heard James wail from inside, snapping him out of his trance.

Sean continued his run for the back door. His hands turned the knob as he yanked on the door. Not too surprising, it was locked. He shook it as hard as he could and then began banging on it in frustration.

A resounding *thump* hit his ears from the other side of the door. Sean took several steps back and pulled the pistol from his pants. He clicked the safety on. Gritting his teeth from the impending impact he propelled himself toward the door. The momentum he generated ricocheted him into a bush on the side of the porch. While scrambling to get to his feet, anger replaced the fear in him when he noticed the stubborn door remained closed.

He retrieved the pistol, which had fallen on the welcome mat when he had bounced off the door, and clicked the safety off. He aimed next to the doorknob like he had seen people do in movies. He fired once and then kicked the door.

His look of surprise, that it worked, matched the stunned expressions of James and the beast at his sudden appearance.

Not wasting any time, Sean raised the weapon and lined up its sights to the monster's head. He squeezed the trigger and felt elation when the beast's skull jerked as the shell passed through it. Without a sound, the creature toppled off his friend.

"Hell yeah! Man, thank God! It… It almost had me!" James sputtered as Sean helped him to his feet.

"Is Elizabeth okay? Where's she at?" Sean frantically asked him while slipping the weapon back into his pants.

"She's out cold in the living room," James said as he led Sean from the kitchen, "That little zombie clocked her a good one."

"Wait, did you just call that thing a zombie?" Sean asked.

"Well yeah, that's what they are," James said with certainty.

"Oh God… No!" Sean's thoughts slipped away as he knelt down next to Elizabeth's still form. He cradled her head in his hands, brushing the hair off of her face and shaking his head at the whelps that were forming on her face.

"Is she—" James began.

"She's breathing, but she looks horrible," Sean cut him off, "I saw you shoulder slam that thing—"

"Zombie. Damn it, it's a zombie!" James countered.

"Zombie, whatever the hell you wanna' call it," Sean continued, "I saw you get it off her. Thank you. I just wanna', you know, thank you."

James quietly regarded Sean. The younger kid hadn't torn his gaze away from Elizabeth since he saw her. The older boy glanced out of the shattered window and uneasily kept vigil over the pair, giving his friends what privacy he could.

A series of hisses and guttural sounding barks had his full attention on the lawn. Another fiend, even larger than the first one he saw, had now joined the group. Spittle flew from its mouth as it snarled at the rest of the creatures. With shaking muscles it lashed out in fury at everything around it.

The other large beast roared and charged the newcomer. James watched in awe as the larger beast took an incredibly powerful right hook to the jaw. Pieces of grey flesh and putrid, yellowish, bone were ripped away by the blow. In response to the assault, the larger creature grabbed the other one in a bear hug and began squeezing. With screeches of delight the smaller creatures swarmed closer to the two brutes to watch the carnage.

"Sean," James whispered just loud enough for his friend to hear, "Two of the giant ones are fighting. We have got to go before the winner decides to tear this house down!"

Sean nodded his agreement and stood up, careful to ease Elizabeth's head to the ground first. He looked around the living room and spied a woven afghan blanket sitting next to an old, standup sewing machine. He rushed over and grabbed it saying, "We need to make something to carry her in. Find something we can use as poles!"

"I'm on it!" James said, rushing out of the room.

With a quick shake, Sean spread out the blanket next to the unconscious girl. He carefully folded it in half to increase its strength and started searching around the living room for something to help carry her.

"I got something!" announced James as he returned.

Sean smiled wide when he saw that his friend was carrying two shovels. Taking one of them, he twisted and yanked until the head came loose. Kneeling down next to the afghan, Sean then rolled some of its side around the shovel handle. James, understanding what Sean's intention was, assembled his in the same way.

"We'll have ta' hold the ends tight or she'll fall," James said.

"Yeah, so we'll be as careful as we can. Help me pick her up and set her on the blanket," Sean murmured.

The two boys easily lifted the much lighter girl onto their makeshift stretcher. Sean grabbed the handles and gathered up as much of the blanket as he could. He faced her and was glad James didn't complain about taking the lead position. In a few moments the boys were shuffling along in shadows, carrying their friend as comfortably as they could.

As Sean heard the continuing battle between the two brutes, an old song his mother used to sing him came to mind. The once comforting tune now held an eerie tone to its lyrics. Still, he couldn't help humming it as James navigated the alleyways; leaving the hissing and roaring of the fiends behind them.

Girls and boys, come out to play,
The moon doth shine as bright as day;

Leave your supper, and leave your sleep,
And come with your friends into the street.
Come with a whoop, come with a call,
Come with good will or not at all.
Up the ladder and down the wall,
A halfpenny roll will serve us all.
You find milk, and I'll find flour,
And we'll have pudding in half an hour.

"Hey, Sean?"

"Yeah?"

"If you're gonna hum something, hum something that doesn't spook the shit out of me."

"Beware of false prophets, which come to you in sheep's clothing, but inwardly they are ravening wolves. Ye shall know them by their fruits. Do men gather grapes of thorns, or figs of thistles? Even so every good tree bringeth forth good fruit; but a corrupt tree bringeth forth evil fruit. A good tree cannot bring forth evil fruit, neither can a corrupt tree bring forth good fruit. Every tree that bringeth not forth good fruit is hewn down, and cast into the fire. Wherefore by their fruits ye shall know them."

- Matthew 7:15-20

HEIGH-HO, THE DERRY-O . . .

His breathing was labored. Each intake of air seemed to exit his lungs in a hacking cough. More than once, Matt was sure that Justin was going to pass out from the unaccustomed pace.

Justin, had he known what his friend was thinking, would readily agree with his assessment of the situation. Between the cigarettes he had smoked over the last several years and the constant influx of booze in his system, he was more surprised than either Matt or Father Murray with his ability to keep up.

Thomas couldn't hide his glares of disgust at Justin. If it was up to him he would have left the fat drunken bastard back at the church. Not that he was doing much better. His back ached painfully from the long run and he wished he had bothered to grab his pain pills before they all fled the house.

Thomas could only vaguely recall those last few horrifying moments. Jacqueline reaching out for him, waving that blood spewing stump in his face. He felt bile rise in his throat thinking of it. At least the monster had concentrated solely on her during its attack.

Matt, at the front of the group, had slowly begun to circle back toward the church. Leaving that woman to die was one thing, but abandoning Sean was something he couldn't live with. He knew the chances of the kid still being at the church, let alone even being alive, was a million to one… But he just couldn't risk leaving him like that.

Up ahead, a small tool shed caught Matt's eye. He slowed down and motioned for the others to stop. Keeping a wary eye out, he slowly covered the ground to the building. After looking in a window he waved Justin and Father Murray over to him as he entered the structure.

Matt slunk down in a corner away from the window as the others entered behind him. Father Murray shut the door and leaned against the wall, rubbing his lower back. Justin collapsed on the floor and continued to cough wildly. Father Murray shot a warning look toward Matt, who shook his head in acknowledgement of the gesture.

"Slow and easy, man. Slow and easy," Matt said, "Just try to calm down."

"He should stay here and rest," Thomas suggested, "You and I can find a car and then we'll come back for him."

Matt and Justin were both shaking their heads as the priest spoke.

"No, we stay together!" Matt said firmly.

Father Murray swallowed a nasty retort and nodded in agreement. As soon as he had some reliable transportation, he would leave these two assholes on the side of the road. Until he was safely behind the wheel though, he would be agreeable to their wishes.

"You're right, of course," Father Murray said, "We do need to stay together. I'm just concerned that if we run into any more of those beasts—"

"I understand your concerns. Now here's mine," Matt cut him off, "I'm not going to leave my friend. And if, IF, some fuckin' monster gets ahold of him I'm gonna' do whatever I can to SAVE him."

The priest's eyes narrowed dangerously as he stared at Matt. Justin, who for the moment was able to keep his coughing under control, was looking back and forth between the other two men.

Matt had his hands up and was pointing at Father Murray as he continued speaking, "Do you understand what I am saying here, FATHER?"

"Matt, there isn't anything he could of—" Justin mumbled.

"And YOU!" Matt turned toward his friend, "Listen to me until this shit's over! Man, just listen to me. Don't second guess me! The next time I tell you to move, just do it!"

"What are you trying to say?" Thomas said with barely disguised fury, completely ignoring Matt's conversation with Justin.

"I'm not tryin' to say anything. I believe you know exactly what I mean!" Matt spewed at Thomas.

Justin was wide eyed as he watched Matt. He had never seen his friend so pissed at someone without fists being thrown. He wasn't sure what Father Murray had done, or what Matt thought he had done, but it must have been bad.

"You're not any kind of leader! I will not stand here and—"

Matt suddenly shook his hand at the priest for silence. He half turned his head toward the window and listened intently. He motioned for everyone to get down and placed his ear against the metal siding of the shed.

Thomas clamped his mouth shut, biting off a round of heated words that were boiling up inside him. He understood the necessity for silence when he heard shuffling sounds from outside.

Matt took a quick inventory of the tools in the shed. He smiled when his gaze fell across a pickaxe in the corner. He slid over to it and inspected the tool. No rust, clean handle, it would do nicely. He stood and hefted the weapon in front of him.

He nodded towards the tools on the wall as he moved into position next to the door. He kept staring at the closed door as the other two men grabbed tools. A look over his shoulder revealed that Justin had grabbed a roofing hammer and the priest a hand axe.

Thomas chanced a glance out the window and saw two small forms lurking along the fence line by the alley. He hastily ducked back down, confident that they did not see him. He held up two fingers on his left hand and pointed in the direction they were coming from.

A few tense moments passed. They all heard footsteps just beyond the thin metal walls; footsteps that stopped next to the door. Thomas slowly put his hand on the knob and looked towards Matt for confirmation. Matt took a deep breath and nodded his head.

Father Murray flung the door open as Matt rushed out, the head of the pickaxe leading the way. Sean and James were on the ground before Matt could stop his initial assault. Luckily, the blunt head of the pickaxe had caught them in their lower torsos only, forcing the air from their lungs.

"Holy shit! Are you okay?" Matt dropped his weapon and kneeled next to the boys. Both of them held their wounded guts but had smiles on their faces.

"Sean! James!" Father Murray exclaimed as he came out of the shed, "Thank the Lord!"

Justin couldn't hold back his tears when he saw the kids lying on the wet grass. He rushed out and scooped up Sean and held him close. The boy was still trying to gain control of his lungs enough to draw breath, but he returned the embrace. Matt helped James to his feet while saying, "You don't know how good it is to see you kids!"

James, unable to talk, pointed towards the direction of the alley and shook his finger vigorously. Matt scrutinized the area and gasped when he saw a younger girl stretched out on an afghan next to the fence. He rushed toward the child and ordered, "Justin, give me a hand!"

The former pastor let go of Sean and headed toward Matt. He picked up his pace when he saw the helpless teen on the ground. Matt was giving her a cursory examination when he arrived at her side.

"What happened to her?" Matt asked the boys.

"Zombie punched her. Knocked her out," wheezed James.

"Before that, the back of her head was slammed pretty hard against the floor," Sean explained, "I think she's hurt bad."

"Zombie? What the fuck is wrong with you?" Matt snorted toward James.

"Don't press it, Matt. He's stuck on calling them zombies and, well… I guess that's as good of a label as any," Sean replied as he knelt down next to Elizabeth.

"She's not waking up," Justin slurred, "Musta' been a bad hit."

The priest rolled his eyes. Between the fat, out of shape drunk and sleeping beauty they were all going to get killed. He gruffly cleared his throat and when everyone looked at him he spoke, "We have to get out of town. We have to find something large enough for all of us to fit in. I said it earlier, but now there is no other option. Matt, you and I need to leave them here and bring transportation back."

Matt stood and marched toward Father Murray. Justin interposed himself between the two men and put a hand on each of their chests. His shoulders were slumped and the sad expression on his face took the fire out of Matt's anger toward the cowardly priest.

"Matt, he's right. I know it sucks, but he's right about this," Justin sighed, "We can stay in the shed until you get back."

Matt looked passed his friend at the priest. He couldn't be positive, but he thought the bastard was actually smirking at him. He let another wave of hate pass through him and did his best to give Justin a comforting smile.

"Yeah, he's right. I'm so sorry, man," Matt replied, "Are you sure you got this?"

Justin looked at the two boys. His gaze settled on Sean and he smiled. He knew the kid was tough. He also knew there was something about him that set him apart from the other kids he had seen. He just couldn't put his finger on it.

"We got this. Get out of here and hurry back," he said to Matt, then to the boys, "Let's get her inside the shed."

Thomas and Matt watched as the door to the shed closed. The fallen priest and former Marine headed off toward the center of town at a jog.

"For the last time, I'm sure the keys are in it," Father Murray hissed through his teeth, "Mister Clarkson always leaves them there in case his son needs the truck!"

"Okay, you drive and I'll take shotgun," Matt commanded.

The priest cursed under his breath as Matt bolted for the old truck. He had enough of this arrogant prick barking orders at him. Since they had left the alley, it had gotten worse. Thomas smiled when he thought of how much better off he would be when he could make his own way.

They moved fast. Matt strode around the front of the truck to enter the passenger side while Thomas sprinted straight for the driver seat. Father Murray cranked the engine and it sputtered to life.

The old beaten up green Ford handled much better than it looked and soon they were nearing the alley where the kids and Justin were hiding. Matt breathed a sigh of relief when Thomas pulled up next to the shed door.

The former Marine got out of the truck and froze after only moving a few feet. All along the alley from the direction they had just come from was crawling with the small child-beasts.

"Stay inside!" Matt shouted as he quickly jumped back into the truck.

Matts sudden yell and movement caused the priest to jump in his seat. As Matt slammed the door closed, Father Murray saw rapid movement behind them through the rearview mirror.

"What the hell?!" he screeched as three of the little monsters leapt into the bed of the truck. He stomped on the gas pedal and careened down the alley.

Matt snatched the hand axe up from the seat where Thomas had laid it and waited to fend off the creatures attacks. The movement of the vehicle, coupled with the priest's wild driving, caused the fiends to slide around the bed. Unable to get traction, one of the creatures was flung off the side as the priest turned onto the blacktop.

Thomas, still watching the action from the rearview mirror, got an idea. He risked a glance over to Matt. He wasn't wearing his seatbelt. He could have taken a few more seconds to tell him what he had planned, but he knew how fast the little monsters could move. He gritted his teeth and slammed on the breaks.

Just as he hoped, the remaining monsters were hurled against the cab, their momentum carrying them up and over the hood. From the passenger seat he saw Matt had been thrown into the dash and the hand axe had embedded itself in his left shoulder.

His skull had smacked the windshield pretty hard and he felt every inch of the blade as the axe sank into his shoulder. He saw the creatures fly over the cab and heard loud *thumps* on the hood. He twisted around to face forward and Thomas gunned the engine again.

"Are you okay?" the priest muttered.

"Yeah," Matt responded while pulling the blade out of his shoulder, "I'm fuckin' right as rain you mother fucker!"

Father Murray turned his face toward him and smiled, "It had to be done."

Matt drew his right arm back for a swing at Father Murray but was interrupted by a loud roar behind them. He noticed the priest's eyes widen as the clergyman pushed down harder on the gas.

Looking behind him he saw something right out of his nightmares. Racing behind the truck, maybe only three or four yards away, was a beast the size of a midsize sedan. Huge muscles flexed and rippled all over its body as it charged them. Hellish red pupils blazed out from sunken eye sockets and seemed to focus on Matt.

"Go! Go! Go!" yelled the former Marine.

"What do you think I'm doing?!" screamed Thomas.

Slowly the truck pulled away from the brute. It stopped in the middle of the road and roared a long sound of hate and maliciousness that echoed through the night. Matt pulled his shirt off and examined his wound. Blood was flowing freely from the wicked gash and he felt light headed.

"Head back to the shed," he ordered as he pressed his shirt against his injury.

"No way! There is NO way they survived those... THINGS!" Father Murray gruffly said.

"I said turn this around and pick them up!" Matt leaned forward and swooned.

"You are in no condition to tell me what to do!" the priest laughed, "How long do you think you'd last against one of them now? Not long, that's for sure! Now shut up and try to relax!"

Father Thomas expected more of an argument and the silence that followed surprised him. He looked at his passenger and sighed when he saw he had passed out. Using his right arm he put more pressure on the wound as he rocketed out of town. He would do what he could to save him. He might need him later.

It could have lasted seconds or it could of lasted hours. Time had become jumbled for everyone in the shed after the truck sped away. Justin's hand was about to push it open when Matt yelled his warning. In horror, they all watched as the truck sped away with a horde of monsters chasing after it.

After the last of the creatures sped by, the small group fled the questionable safety of the shed. Running from the alley to blacktop, they could hear the roars of one of the larger monsters echoing through the streets.

After searching for several heart pounding minutes, the group found an unlocked car with the keys in the ignition. After making sure Elizabeth was comfortable in the back seat, Justin and the two boys crammed in front.

"Head to Clydes!" Sean suggested with James nodding in affirmation.

"Sounds like a good place to start," mumbled the fallen pastor as he pulled onto the street.

The drive through town was eerie. It was quiet except for the droning of the engine and the occasional scream of pain or roar of fury. Justin felt a wave of panic as a herd of the smaller creatures stormed out of an alley behind them and gave chase.

Looking at them as they faded away into the rearview, he felt an overwhelming sadness. Even though they no longer resembled children they still looked so small and frail. He could almost still make out certain individuals among the mob. They were some of the nicest and sweetest kids he had ever met. All of them so meek—

Meek, he thought, *My God. They are all children and meek!*

His mind raced as he thought back to the events of the last few days. Had it happened? Did the rapture actually just happen? Tears fell from his eyes with the sudden realization that it must have. The meek had indeed inherited the Earth. They had inherited the Earth with blood and carnage, not in the way everyone thought they might.

He glanced at the boys next to him, both sleeping uneasily now, and wept even more. If this was the End Times, there was no hope for any of them. Justin gripped the steering wheel even harder. His nails dug into it and his fingers began to throb painfully.

He finally loosened his grip as he guided the car to the gravel road that led to Clyde's house. He was relieved to see that none of his friend's vehicles were gone as he put the car into park in front of one of the small guest cabins.

He shut off the engine and again looked at the three children sleeping close to him. He didn't want to bring them out of their dreams back into this nightmare, but he had no choice. He gently shook Sean until the boy sat up and looked at him.

"Wake up your friend, son. We're home."

He knew something was wrong the moment they started waking up. He didn't have to see the janitor get ripped to pieces to know that hell had come to Earth. He didn't have to see the sharp claws and needle fangs forming on the children to know that some form of demons had invaded their bodies. He knew he had to hide, so he fled for the safety of his apartment.

He had closed the deadbolt and shoved his table up against the door when he got home and then pulled the couch over for an extra barricade. Screams cascaded all around him. Among the screams was something even more terrifying to him, the sounds of children laughing.

Mister Dabner collapsed on the couch in exhaustion and

fear. His breathing coming in ragged gasps and he felt pain in his throat and in his chest. He leaned back and closed his eyes, just trying to steady his nerves.

He was thrown across the room as his door exploded inward. The table shattered under the heavy blow of something huge that burst through. As he picked himself up off the ground he saw the beast.

Almost seven feet tall, with greyish skin falling from its muscular frame, the beast plucked him into the air by his shoulders. He stared into a bestial face that seemed almost familiar; a face that once might have been—

"Judy!" he gasped.

The creature roared in his face and roughly slammed him against the wall. He felt pain all over his body as ribs exploded and his legs began shaking uncontrollably. A giggle caused him to stiffen and forced him to look up.

Climbing over the shoulder from the back of the monster was a small blonde haired little baby girl. Her face was almost angelic as she crawled toward him. He smiled when she got close. She smiled back at him. He didn't like what he saw. His screams from seeing her razor sharp teeth ended in a gurgle when the fiend ripped his throat open.

The last thing Jake Dabner ever saw were the monsters feeding each other his flesh. The larger one being exceptionally gentle as it dangled the gory tidbit just within reach of its daughter. Judy and Melissa, or the monsters that now warped their skin, took their time with the meal.

CHILDREN OF ENOCH

CHILDREN OF ENOCH
THE REAPING
OF SORROWS

AVAILABLE 2015

TEASER...

The screams of Anna spurred him on to speeds greater than he ever believed possible. Mercifully, those screams were abruptly cut short. He was thankful for that. He was also thankful that he hadn't been a target during the ambush by the clever little creepers.

Luke dared a look behind him as he ran. A mob of the beasts slinked around the bodies of his sisters, fighting each other over their flesh. One of the grey skinned creatures ripped Clair's head off of her torso before he could avert his gaze.

Luke ran on, fighting down tears and the urge to vomit. He ran until he felt his lungs burning. Then he ran some more. He ran until his bare feet were bleeding, leaving a crimson trail for anyone, or anything, to follow. Then he ran some more. He ran until his vision clouded over and the ringing in his ears sounded like the roar of cannons. He slipped on something and felt himself falling, but the ground never caught him…

He awoke sometime during the night to a dog licking the bottom of his left foot. He opened his eyes, but couldn't remember why he was laying in the middle of the road. He stared up at the night sky and could no longer hold back his tears.

They exploded from him in great bouts. Long mournful sobs echoed through the wilderness on each side of him. He cried, even as the rough tongue of the dog moved to his other foot. His dad had told him once that a dog licking a wound would help it heal, but he didn't know how much truth was in that. A thought came to him, *How can an animal that eats its own shit have a healthy mouth?*

The thought of that suddenly repulsed him and he jerked his leg up and away from the dog. He was too surprised to even scream when he suddenly felt claws dig into his leg as it was pulled back down, accompanied by a deep growl.

For the first time since he opened his eyes he took in his surroundings. Down at his feet was a lone creeper. Its grey mottled skin absorbing much more moonlight than it was reflecting. He began to shake as a wave of panic flooded his body.

The monster continued to lick the bottom of his foot; Its rough tongue slowly peeling skin away from him, causing blood to flow again. The creature moaned softly as it tasted the warm liquid and began to lick even harder. *It's treating me like a fucking lollipop,* his brain screamed, *I'm nothing more than a Goddamned fleshsicle for this thing!*

He tensed his body and prepared to use the last bit of his strength to kick the child-beast. Flexing his muscles he sent his leg as hard as he could against the side of its head. The blow landed solidly and the creeper was flung off him.

He started to scamper to his feet, but the demon was on him faster than he could imagine. It rammed him face down onto the hard pavement and howled in his ear. Luke closed his eyes and silently pleaded, to whatever goodness remained in the world, for a fast death.

CRACK! The noise startled him. He felt the monster stiffen for a brief moment and then it toppled off of him. Luke rolled over on his back and pulled himself into a sitting position.

Turning his head to the left he saw a figure emerging from the woods on the side of the road. As the stranger stepped into the moonlight Luke's face cracked into the first smile he had in over a month. Coming toward him was a priest carrying a pistol.

"Thank you! God… Thank you! I was sure I was dead but now—"

CRACK! The same noise that saved him heralded the end of Luke's life. Father Murray slowly lowered the weapon, stepping in closer to make sure he had hit the kid in the head.

"What the fuck!"

Thomas sighed and turned to face Matt, "He was bitten. You know what happens."

"He's just a fucking kid! I didn't see the damn thing bite him! Why'd you kill him?!" Matt screamed as he limped from the woods on a makeshift crutch.

The priest pointed at the corpse's feet, "The monster was licking him so hard he was bleeding. Saliva and blood, bite or not, that thing's fluids were mixed with his."

"We don't know if that's how it works," Matt said, "We don't know how any of this works!"

"I know that when we tried to save Jacob all it took was the thing spitting in his mouth!" Thomas shot back, "Do you really want to argue about this out here?"

Matt glared at the priest, but kept silent. Bending over, he examined the teenagers feet. The creature's spittle was all over them. Matt straightened himself and looked the body up and down a few times.

"Are you ready to get back yet?" Thomas asked with a smirk as he casually strolled towards the woods.

Matt looked from the body at his feet to the monster retreating in front of him. He briefly entertained the thought of clubbing him to death with his crutch.

"Sorry, kid," he murmured as he followed Father Murray, "I have a feeling that bastard actually did you a favor."

ABOUT THE AUTHOR

Edward Gehlert started his career in the publishing industry in 2000 as a copy editor. Since that time he has written more than 25 books. These works were military base guides, welcome guides, and business guides. He has also written countless articles that have appeared in various media outlets. This is his first published work of fiction and he is busy working on several more projects in other genres.

Edward is the Editorial Manager for F&M Publishing, a position he has held for the past five years, and prior to that he worked in the emergency services field as a 911 operator and then as a police officer.

Edward Gehlert has always been fascinated by the power of the written word. From a young age he has been carried along on magical journeys, all of which were weaved by skilled storytellers. His dream, now realized, was to one day join them.

Edward currently resides in Owensville, Missouri with his wife, Eva, and son, Wayde.

Check out these other great titles from New Babel Books:

The Apocalypse of Enoch Series
"Rapture"
"Scourge"
"Desolation"

Abyss Walker titles

Core Series
"The Plea of Apollisian"
"The Trial of Innocence"
"Darrion-Quieness"
"Death of Kings"
"Tides of Winter"
"Return of the Father"

The Wererat's Tale Series
"The Wererat's Tale-Of Rats and Men"
"The Wererat's Tale-Ring of the Nonul"
"The Wererat's Tale-The Collar of Perdition"

White Wraith Series
"White Wraith-The Escape"
"White Wraith-Lock of Requ"
"White Wraith-Malestrom Serpents"

For additional NBB titles, visit: www.newbabelbooks.com

www.ingramcontent.com/pod-product-compliance
Lightning Source LLC
Chambersburg PA
CBHW060054260626
47160CB00005B/1679